She tugged the photo of herself and her twin up for Adam's inspection, pointed to one twin then the other. "That's Ophelia, and that's me. Josie."

Confusion registered in his expression. "Who's Josie?"

"Josie is me, pal. The woman who is kicking you out of here before we wake my baby."

"For the baby's sake, I'll go, but just so we can sort this whole mess through somewhere else."

"Agreed." She ushered him into the hallway, pulling the bedroom door firmly shut after them.

"And for the record, ma'am..." He leaned down close until his face loomed before hers, his eyes demanding her total focus. "That little boy asleep in that crib in there—"

She held her breath.

"—is *my* baby."

Books by Annie Jones

Love Inspired

April in Bloom #343
Somebody's Baby #411

Steeple Hill Café

Sadie-in-Waiting
Mom Over Miami
The Sisterhood of the Queen Mamas

ANNIE JONES,

winner of a Holt Medallion for Southern Themed Fiction and *Houston Chronicle*'s Best Christian Fiction Author of 1999, grew up in a family who loved to laugh, eat and talk—often all at the same time. They instilled in her the gift of sharing through words and humor, and the confidence to go after her heart's desire (and to act fast if she wanted the last chicken leg). A former social worker, she feels called to be a "voice for the voiceless" and has carried that calling into her writing by creating characters often overlooked in our fast-paced culture—from seventy-somethings who still have a zest for life to women over thirty with big mouths and hearts to match. Having moved thirteen times during her marriage, Annie is currently living in rural Kentucky with her husband and two children.

Somebody's Baby
Annie Jones

Steeple
Hill®

Published by Steeple Hill Books™

STEEPLE HILL BOOKS

Steeple
Hill®

ISBN-13: 978-0-373-87447-7
ISBN-10:   0-373-87447-2

SOMEBODY'S BABY

What do you think? If a man owns a hundred sheep, and one of them wanders away, will he not leave the ninety-nine on the hills and go to look for the one that wandered off? And if he finds it, I tell you the truth, he is happier about that one sheep than about the ninety-nine that did not wander off. In the same way your Father in heaven is not willing that any of these little ones should be lost.

—*Matthew* 18:12-14

For Elijah Dobben and Riley Davis, the two newest babies in the Jones family tree. You already have the blessing of wonderful parents who love you so dearly, but a legacy of faith that will serve you all your days.

And remember when they speak of your "Great" Aunt Annie, that's not just a label, it's a promise! Really. I already have toys in my closet for when you come to visit.

Prologue

"What is your secret, Miss Josie?"

"Secret?" Josie Redmond wiped her hands on the long white bib-apron covering her pink T-shirt and black jeans. She swallowed hard to push down a bitter lump of anxiety. Her gaze darted from the face of the man sitting at the counter to the huge glass window with the swirling red lettering spelling out the name of her business—Josie's Home Cookin' Kitchen.

Did her customers know she hadn't taken in enough money this month to pay her business loan to the Mt. Knott First National Bank? That the bleak downturn in business for the Carolina Crumble Pattie Factory had taken its toll on not only her customer base but also threatened to rob her of a very essential ingredient to her success? Or had someone gotten wind of the fact that her twin sister had been trying to contact her?

Just thinking of what her sister wanted left Josie feeling jumpy as a cat, fearing for everything she held dear.

Her eyes went to the far wall of her diner, the one she had painted with special black paint, virtually turning the whole side of the room into a giant chalkboard. She had meant it to keep young people from carving their initials on the tables and to allow children something to busy themselves with while their parents lingered over the last bites of dessert. But somewhere along the line, it had turned into a town message board. A place where people left notes to friends, reminders of upcoming events and, in a segment sectioned off by vines drawn in pink and green chalk, a prayer request list.

"Please remember Millie Tillson's oldest girl— baby due any day."

"Traveling mercies for Agnes and Virgil."

"For our children and teachers as the new school year begins."

Some farmer in the midst of a dry summer spell had simply scrawled in an earnest, oversize script: "RAIN."

And of course: "Pray for the Burdetts. Our jobs. The whole of Mt. Knott."

All summer Josie had been praying about all the things that got posted on her wall, as well as for the welfare of all the people she cared about in her adopted hometown of Mt. Knott, South Carolina. But her deepest concerns remained between her and the Lord, not something she wanted thrown out to feed the small-town rumor mill.

"Secret?" She laughed and tossed her head, knowing it would make her strawberry-blond ponytail bounce and give her an even younger appearance than her twenty-four years. "What secret?"

The older of the two long-past-middle-age regulars sitting on the stools at the lunch counter lifted his fork with the last bite of cherry pie for his answer. "Go-oo-od stuff."

The other man leaned in on his elbows, his deep-set eyes twinkling. "When you going to marry me, Sweetie Pie?"

All the men over a certain age in town called Josie Sweetie Pie. They said it was because she was sweeter than a baby's kiss and cuter than a bug's ear and whatever other cornpone phrase they could toss out to make her laugh. But really, they called her that because Josie Redmond, who otherwise thought herself a most unremarkable young woman, made the best pies in seven counties.

Everybody said so. In fact, more than one person just passing through town had told her that if she could ever figure out a way to market the unique pastry to the masses, she'd make a mint. Right now, Josie couldn't even afford to *buy* a mint, she thought, letting her eyes trail to the empty candy dish by the cash register.

"You? You're not her type, Warren." The more

rough-around-the-edges of the two men looked into his coffee mug and grinned. "It's *me* she's going to marry."

"And spend the rest of my life trying to stay ahead of your appetite for pie, Jed? No, thanks." Josie teased the white-haired man in striped overalls and a short-sleeved plaid shirt. "I am on to you two. Always proposing and slopping sugar all over me like that when I know all you really want is to sweet-talk your way to a second slice on the house."

The older men laughed.

"Best pie I ever tasted," Warren pushed his plate forward, the fork rattling over the streaks of cherry pie filling adding to the simple pattern. "But don't go and tell my wife."

"About you proposing?" Josie took the plate away.

"Naw, she knows all about that. Don't tell her what I said about your pie. She thinks I only come here to eat it because her new job keeps her too busy to bake."

At the mention of someone having a new job heads turned and the room got real still.

"Part-time at the bowling alley over in Logan-ville. And no, they ain't looking to hire anyone else." Jed raised his head and hollered to everyone all at once. He lowered his head a bit and gave it a slow shake. "Rents shoes to snotty teenagers who don't know they're smarting off to a woman who probably did quality assurance on every Crumble they stuffed into their rude little mouths growing up."

Warren huffed.

Crumble. What an apt word for both the dessert cake and for the condition that the poor management at the factory—which everyone also called "the Crumble"—had left the town in. All those hopes, all those plans, all those lives, crumbled like the crisp brown-sugar topping of the "coffee cake with the coffee right in it."

Josie stared at the empty plates in her hands. "You know, y'all, I think I might have short-changed you a bit on the size of your pie slices this morning, let me get you a second sliver on the house."

She would never make her bank payment doing business like this, but Josie couldn't help it. The whole town had felt the sting since the Burdett family had had to make cuts at the factory. Nineteen jobs gone already and another half dozen on the line. It might not seem like a lot but in a town of less than two thousand, counting kids and retirees, it made a palpable impact.

What a great time to try to open a business, Josie thought as she picked up the clear plastic lid on the pie stand. But then, timing had never been her strong suit.

Josephine Sunshine Redmond had been born almost a half hour after her identical twin sister, Ophelia Rainbow. That led their free spirit of a mother to announce, often and all their lives, that this meant Ophelia embraced life, chased it, was unstoppable in going after what she wanted while Josie was a plodding, methodical, reluctant old soul.

All their lives her sister had rushed headlong into one, uh, *adventure* after another while Josie tried to find comfort and like-minded people wherever the family's lifestyle landed them. Whenever they had arrived in a new place, chasing anything from freedom of expression—meaning a place where their mother could sell her art at local shops and craft fairs—to seeking out new experiences, which could mean *anything,* Josie had looked around for a nice, friendly church.

That was one new experience her mother just couldn't understand. So when Josie announced she had given her life to Christ at seventeen, the family had left her behind with her grandmother right here in Mt. Knott to finish her senior year of high school and find her own way in life. Josie had done just that. She had gone to work for the Burdetts and used their college-payback program to get an associate's degree in business administration. Then, at the beginning of this summer, when she knew her job was about to be phased out, she'd used the general goodwill toward her in the community to open the diner. It was early August now. They'd been open a full three months. Josie still had the community's goodwill but not their financial support. No one had any money to spare!

Her sister had had her own set of new experiences, mostly involving men and substance abuse. She came to visit Josie from time to time, and Josie tried to influence her for the good, but it never lasted.

A day or two of saying she was going to change was always followed by nights of partying and the inevitable taking off for parts unknown. The visits had stopped entirely a year ago when Ophelia had dropped a bombshell—well, a baby boy, actually—on her sister's doorstep. She asked Josie to care for the child for a few weeks while she got herself together, then disappeared.

Now Ophelia was trying to get in touch. After a year of loving the little boy she had named Nathan, a Biblical name that meant gift, Josie was now afraid that her rotten timing had reared its head again and she was about to lose her son forever.

Beep. Beep.

The familiar bleating of their local mailman's scooter horn jerked Josie out of her worried state.

She looked up and blinked, then looked at the two pieces of pie in her hands. She must have sliced them and plopped them on plates without even thinking about what she was doing.

"Here you go, boys." She plunked the free food down on the counter and rushed toward the door and out onto the sidewalk in front of the diner.

"Got a letter for you, Miss Josie." Bob "Bingo" Barnes waved a large white envelope. "Looks important."

"From a lawyer?" Josie asked. Her fingers trembled as she reached for the suspect packet.

Bingo, a big man with bad knees who always delivered the mail on a small red scooter with an orange flag sticking out of the back, blinked at her. "I don't think it's from a lawyer."

But now that Josie had suggested it, the man clearly wanted to hang around and make sure.

Josie fingered the name on the return label, then glanced over her shoulder trying to calculate which would draw more attention. Should she stand here on the street in full view of everyone, take the bad news and have the whole town know her business in a matter of minutes? Or rush inside past all her regulars and hide in the kitchen and raise all kinds of concerns and speculations that would follow her for days, maybe years to come?

"Better to just get it over with," she muttered.

"Ma'am?" Bingo leaned forward, his eyes peering at her and his frown overemphasizing the fullness of his jowls.

R-r-r-rip. Josie worked her finger under the flap. She held her breath and slowly slid the papers out.

"Everything all right, Miss Josie?"

She was a struggling single mom, abandoned by her own family. Her business was teetering on the brink. Her town's economic base was literally crumbling beneath it. And yet…

She stared in disbelief at the papers in her hands. The paperwork signed by Ophelia relinquished parental rights and included a birth certificate naming his biological father so Josie could find the man and secure his approval for her to go forward with Nathan's legal adoption.

To the rest of the world Josie Redmond was just a plain little pie maker in a pickle, but when she saw the contents of that envelope she knew she was blessed beyond all belief. And all she could say was, "You know, Bingo, God is so good. And thanks for asking, because, yes, everything is going to be just fine now."

Chapter One

Two Weeks Later

The South Carolina sky was black. His boots, jeans, T-shirt, all black. They matched Adam Burdett's silent, gleaming Harley—and his mood.

He narrowed his eyes at the simple frame house before him. Though he had grown up around Mt. Knott, this part of the small town was unfamiliar to him. His family had tended to keep to their fancy homes outside of town and didn't interact much with others.

"Bad for business," his father had said. Better to draw a distinct line between employees or potential employees—which is how they saw everyone in town—and friends. Never ask a personal question. Never commit anything more than a name and face to memory. Never offer more than the job description spelled out on paper.

"You do those things," the old man had warned his sons while they stood in the office of his snack food factory, "and it makes it a lot harder to have to fire a person later. And you will have to fire one of them, maybe a lot of them at some point."

According to the letters to the editor in the *Mt. Knott Mountain Laurel and Morning News* that Adam had read when he hit town a few hours ago, the old man had known what he was talking about. A lot of people in town were out of work. Even more were out of patience with the lack of a solution to their plight. A few were pretty close to being thrown out of their homes.

He gritted his teeth and forced the mixed-up emotions in his gut to quiet. On one hand the failure of his father's factory was just what Adam had wanted. On the other...

He gazed at the humble home again and exhaled, long and low. On the other hand, maybe there was something to be said for making connections, for caring about what happened to people once they walked out the factory door. He never had, and look where his callous attitude toward others had led him.

The empty matchbook in his hand rasped against his thumb as he flicked it open to check the address scrawled there. This was it. In this house, illuminated only by the pulsating light of a small-screen TV, Adam would find his son.

His son. The words tripped over his ragged nerves

like a fingernail strummed over taut barbwire. Adam
Burdett had a son.

He hadn't even known it until yesterday morning
when a slick-haired private investigator had weaseled
his way into Adam's office with the news and an un-
thinkable demand—that Adam sign away all rights
to his child, sight unseen. There was about as much
chance of that happening as there was of that P.I. ever
suggesting such a notion again in this lifetime.

Adam hadn't belted the guy. But then again, he
hadn't needed to.

Adam might look like nothing more than a good
ol' boy, redneck rodeo rider with beef for brains, but
looks, like too many other things in life, could be deceiving. Raised in a family of wealth and influence
by a mother who treasured the value of an education,
none of the Burdett boys were dummies. They could
put thoughts and words together as well as they could
fists and flesh.

And Adam had proven as much and then some to
that paper-waving P.I. Give up his son for adoption
and never look back? Adam huffed out a hard breath.
Uh-uh. He'd never do to any child what had been
done to him.

He folded his arms over his chest, fit one well-worn
cowboy boot over the other at the ankle and leaned
back against his parked Harley. Everything Adam had
become in this life—and everything he had failed to
become—he owed first to his adoptive mother, who

had never treated him like anything but her own child and next to his own father. Whoever that was.

He knew who it *wasn't*. It wasn't his adoptive father, Conner Burdett, the father of Adam's three brothers. *Adopted* brothers. It shouldn't have been important to add the "adopted" part. Adam had never felt it mattered to his mother, but to the others?

The long-legged and fair-haired Burdett boys claimed Adam as their own even though Adam's broad, muscular build, dark eyes and angular features told differently. The family never spoke of it outright, but Adam sensed the subtle differences. He knew the gnawing ache of never feeling sure that he truly belonged.

To the outside world, at least, Adam was just one of the wolf pack of Burdett boys. A picture flashed in his mind of the four of them standing on the porch of the huge Burdett home in T-shirts they'd had made with their family nicknames emblazoned on them. Those names not only told of each boy as an individual, but said a lot about the real nature of their relationship in the family.

The oldest son, Burke, was born to the title "Top Dawg" and he lived up to the designation. "Lucky Dawg," Adam's next younger brother, Jason, got his name after a near miss that could have cost him his life, or at least a limb, at the factory. The youngest of the Burdett boys, Cody, earned the name "Hound Dawg" for his notorious talent for trailing girls. It had

hung with the kid even now that he had become the
only Burdett son to marry. It even clung to him when
he became a minister.

All three grown men now shared Conner's lean
build and eyes, which some called blue green, others
green blue. They had straight noses and golden tan
complexions.

Adam glanced at his reflection in the Harley's
side mirror. Dark-brown, hooded eyes stared back
from a face the color of baked red Georgia clay. He
swiped a knuckle at the small bump on the bridge of
his nose and sneered.

If his looks didn't give anyone doubts as to where
Adam honestly fit into the Burdett family they would
have only to hear *his* nickname to figure it all out. His
mother said they'd tagged him with it young because
they could never keep him in one place, that he
shared her wanderlust. Her story rang true enough,
he supposed, but that didn't ease the twinge of pain
he felt every time the man they all knew was not his
father called him by his nickname—"Stray Dawg."

All the old feelings twisted in Adam's gut. He
refused to let a child of his become another stray,
raised by someone who could never fully call the
boy his own. No way. Not possible. And he'd do
anything within his power to keep it from happening—even go crawling back to the scene of his
greatest bravado and worst behavior. Back to Mt.
Knott, if not back to his family.

Not that they'd have him back.

Adam had roared out of Mt. Knott a week after his mother's funeral, with an inheritance in hand, all ties to the family business severed and a hangover that had all but erased the events of his last nights in town.

He hadn't heard from or seen his family now in a year and a half but they had surely heard of him. His new position with a competitor had all but run the Burdett boys out of business. Now in order to do the right thing by his baby, he'd had to come home to a place where he knew he would not be welcome. But he would do it. He'd do anything for this baby he had not yet seen.

He scuffed his boot heel on the pocked driveway as he straightened away from his treasured Harley. He'd waited long enough. It was time to go and claim his heir.

Josie hadn't even bothered to lock up the diner. She had just tossed the keys to the young man who did the dishes and asked him to see to it. The message from the young girl who watched Nathan on Thursday evenings, when Josie stayed open until nine, had been muddled by panic. But two words stood out that had caused Josie to tear off her apron and all but run the two blocks from her business to her small rental house.

"Baby's father."

A shudder worked its way through her body. The man who had the power to grant her the one thing she wanted most in life—the chance to adopt the baby boy she'd loved as her own since his birth—was in her home.

She drew in the smell of coffee and day-old pie clinging to her pale-blue T-shirt and the fluffy white scrunchie holding back her curly hair. She'd had to wait a week to get up the nerve and the funds to hire a private detective to contact the man on the birth certificate. Not that she couldn't have tracked him down herself but, well, just looking at the name made her anxious. Adam Burdett!

She hadn't known him but she certainly knew of him. And in a funny way, what she knew had filled her with what now seemed false confidence.

After all, he was the one who had turned his back on his own family and a whole town. How serious could he be about wanting to play a part in his son's life when he had done that? He was Mr. One-Night Stand. According to her sister, he hadn't even called the next day to say…whatever it is a guy says after an encounter like that.

Josie wouldn't know that kind of thing. She and her sister might be identical twins, but their lifestyles were as different as their personalities. Yin and yang. Their mother, a "free thinker" who couldn't keep a job, didn't want a marriage and seemed always in pursuit of the latest trend in spiritual enlightenment, called them that. Light and dark. Day and night.

Josephine and Ophelia.

Josie snorted out a laugh. Even their names said it all. Josephine sounded sturdy, practical. She worked hard and wanted nothing more than to serve the Lord, make a permanent place to call home, to create a family with a man she could trust and depend upon. And to be the kind of woman he could depend upon in return.

"He's in your bedroom," the sitter whispered the last word as Josie hit the front door of her house.

Josie gave the girl a reassuring nod and headed down the hallway. If she could afford a house with more than one bedroom, he'd be in the nursery, but since the crib was in her room, she had expected to find him there. She pulled in one long breath, peered into the dim room, illuminated by only a soft glowing light on her dresser. She stole a quick peek at her sleeping baby, then pushed open her door with one hand, ready to do battle. "I don't know what you think you're doing. But if you value your life, you'll get your hands out of my drawers."

He looked as if he was about to swear, but he didn't, though Josie suspected it was more from shock than good manners or morality. He shut the small drawer he'd been peeking into. He peered at her, instead, then his whole face changed. His eyes narrowed. He smirked a bit. "I didn't expect to run into *you* here."

The deep gravel-throated whisper made her shiver. She froze in the shaft of light pouring in from the hallway. Her stomach clenched.

"I'd say you're looking good, but then, you know that, don't you? You always look good." He did not move into the light, remaining just a silhouette against the mirror above her chest of drawers. "Even after all this time and after…everything you've been through. You look as good as the last time I saw you, Ophelia."

Josie blinked in the darkness, hoping her eyes would adjust to sharpen his image. At the same time, she wanted to clear up a few things for him, as well. "Listen, pal, you've made a mistake. I'm not—"

He stepped from the shadows into the muted light.

Josie's mouth hung open, her every sense in that one instant focused on the man who held her future in his big, calloused hands.

He wasn't huge, though he seemed larger than life in presence. His shoulders angled up from a trim waist and western-cut jeans that bunched in furrows over his traditional-style cowboy boots. What she saw of his face, his strong jaw, determined mouth and slightly crooked nose made a compelling, if not classically handsome, image.

He moved in on her, like something powerful and wild sizing up his prey. His eyes glittered.

She pressed her lips together, too angry at his supposition and his presumptive presence to trust herself to speak.

He began to slowly circle her so close that his soft shirtsleeve rasped against her bare elbow.

The man was playing games with her—or more to the point, with Ophelia.

Ophelia liked games. They were her stock and trade. The man was no fool to go on the offensive to try to beat Ophelia at her own impressive bag of tricks. A sucker for excitement and danger, this predatory act might have been just the thing to get Josie's twin to go all liquid and make her easier to negotiate with.

But she wasn't Ophelia. She was smart, practical Josie. The dull one. The mom with a child to protect. This man's act was totally lost on her.

His boots scuffed lightly at the floor.

She tossed her head back, lifted her chin in her best attempt at regal composure. If he wanted to deal with her, it would be as two mature adults, no games, no stooping to base animal attraction to put her at a disadvantage. "Listen, cowboy, I know what you're up to."

His shoulder brushed against the curls trailing down her neck from the knot of hair atop her head.

A wolf, that's what he reminded her of, she decided. "I am not the same woman you shared a bed with a couple years ago."

"Yes, I can see that now."

About time. He'd spent at least one night in tangled passion with her sister, after all. Obviously, that was enough to help him see how very different they were, how very un-Ophelia-like and unappealing to a man like him Josie was.

"Yes, you've made a mistake, all right," she said. "A big one. I am not—"

"I got it. Not the same woman. You think I don't see that?" He slid his gaze over her, quick and businesslike, as if he were sizing up the marbling on a slab of pot roast before he tossed it in his shopping cart.

Marbling. As in fat. She shook her head at where her mind had immediately gone. Of the many ways she had been made to feel inferior to her sister, being a full size larger than Ophelia, was one Josie couldn't shake. And all local jokes about never trusting a skinny cook didn't really ease her discomfort over it, either. Now she couldn't help feeling self-conscious under this man's scrutiny. She found herself folding her arms over a stubborn pout of a tummy no amount of killer crunches had ever diminished.

He put his hand lightly on her back.

Josie gasped. She raised her hand to push him away and found muscles tight as steel beneath her fingertips.

His touch, warm and gentle, almost a reverent caress, belied the strength within the man. She lifted her gaze to his.

"How could I have not seen it? It was clear the moment I laid eyes on you," he murmured. "You aren't the same woman."

"No, I'm not." It sounded almost like an apology, she realized too late. This time she did push his arm away from her.

He let it fall easily to his own side as if she had had no effect on him whatsoever. "And you sure don't look as good as the last time I saw you."

Accustomed as she was to unfavorable comparisons to her sister in the attractiveness department, this man's assessment stung like a backhanded slap to her self-esteem.

She hung her head. "I'm not surprised you'd think—"

He dipped his head and his eyes searched her face. "You look better."

"Better?" she squeaked, cleared her throat, then matched his smoky whisper in depth and volume. "Better?"

"Mmm-hmm." He nodded. "Motherhood becomes you."

She smiled. Maybe this guy wasn't a total jerk after all. He knew who she was and had picked up on the one thing in which she had outshone her vivacious twin. Motherhood did become Josie.

She managed a modest smile. "Thank you for noticing. I know we have a lot to deal with, but it's good to know you can see how important being a mom is to me."

"Oh, yeah, I can just guess how 'important' motherhood is to a girl like you—" a sudden change came over his features; a hardness rang in his tone as he wrung out the rest "—Ophelia."

Yeeoow. Now she knew how those football coaches

felt when the player dumped a tub of ice on them to celebrate a victory! She peeked to make sure that the baby was still sleeping, then turned with a flourish to face this cowboy-biker-Burdett creep. "How can you not know who I am?"

"I could ask the same of you. Do you know who I am?"

"Of course I know who you are," she whispered back, closing in on him to keep her voice from disturbing her child. "You are the man who, if he doesn't get out of my bedroom this instant, will be explaining himself to the whole Mt. Knott Police Department, every last one of them a close personal friend of mine."

His mouth lifted in a one-sided sneer. "I'll just bet."

She spun quietly around to snatch the only picture she had of herself and her twin from on top of her dresser. "I know them all from going to school here. From working year after year alongside their moms and sisters and wives and friends at *your* family's factory. I know them from serving them meals at my own diner."

Confusion registered in his ominous expression. His gaze flicked downward to the framed photo, then up to her face as if asking if she expected him to understand what she wanted to show him.

She tugged it up higher for his inspection. "That's Ophelia." She jabbed her finger at the girl in the forefront of the photo with her hands up and her hair in her counterpart's face. "That's me. Josie."

"Josie?" He shook his head. "Who is Josie?"

"Josie is me, pal. The woman who is kicking you out of here before we wake my baby." She shoved at his shoulder to prompt him to get moving.

"For the baby's sake, I'll go, but just so we can sort this whole mess through somewhere else."

"Agreed." She ushered him into the hallway, pulling the bedroom door firmly shut after them.

"And for the record, ma'am," he said, stopping short in front of her so that she could neither move past him or retreat.

"What?" she asked, trying to sound as brave as she had felt while defending her son.

"For the record…" He leaned down close until his face loomed before hers, his eyes demanding her total focus. "That little boy asleep in that crib in there—"

She held her breath.

"—is *my* baby."

Chapter Two

"Go on home. I'll be all right." This woman, this spitting image of Ophelia Redmond only...softer, gave the babysitter a comforting pat as she nudged the wide-eyed gal out the front door.

Adam stuffed two fingers of each hand into his back jeans pockets and shifted his weight to one leg. Softer or not, that tangle of red-blond curls with the honest eyes and mama-tiger-protecting-her-cub ferocity stood between him and his son. He didn't like that. Did not like that one bit.

And Adam was determined he would not like her, either. He'd come for his son and that left no room for anything but cold indifference toward the woman who wanted him to relinquish his parental rights.

Josie shut the door and turned to him, a smug expression on her pretty face. "I'd ask you if you wanted some coffee, but seeing as you're not staying long enough to—"

"I take it black," he told her. "The coffee, that is. In a mug, not some wimpy little teacup."

Her eyes cut straight through him like two burning coals. They shone with emotion and life that he'd never seen in her twin's gaze. Not that it mattered, of course. As far as he was concerned, Josie Redmond was the enemy.

"And piping hot," he added, enjoying tweaking her anger a bit more than he really should have allowed himself.

She took in one long, deep breath, held it, then let it out, slow—real slow. "Anything else?"

"With sugar."

"Do tell."

"Yep."

"Well, I like mine decaf. Instant decaf." She jerked her head toward the open door to his left. "You'll find everything you need on the counter."

"Me?" He jammed his thumb into his breastbone.

"You want coffee, you make coffee." She put her hand to the wall and kicked her thick white shoes off. "I'm officially off duty, Mr. Burdett."

"Adam," he drawled, hoping it hid his grudging admiration for her unflappable response and her no-nonsense approach.

She reached up and snagged the white hair-holding thingy loose. Spiral curls clung to it as she dragged it downward. She shook her head, her hair tumbling down to brush her straight shoulders. She put her hand behind her neck. "What did you say?"

"Huh?"

"Maybe *I* should make the coffee after all." She narrowed one eye on him. "Wouldn't want to tax you too much, you know, by expecting you to talk *and* handle a kitchen appliance at the same time. Could get tricky."

Adam huffed a hard laugh, more amused than he wanted to admit. "Bet you get a lot of tips with that winning attitude of yours."

"I do all right." She turned and padded into the kitchen.

"I'll just bet you do," he muttered.

"What'd you say?"

"Adam." He strolled into the glaring light of the kitchen and leaned against the cabinet where she was pulling out two coffee mugs. "I asked you to call me Adam. Mr. Burdett is my father."

"I know." She clunked one cup down on the counter.

"Yeah. Of course. Everyone around here knows the Burdetts." He watched her for some sign that she shared his opinion of his family. Why he wanted to find that commonality with her, he didn't know. It just seemed, standing here in this small space with her, that it sure would be nice to have a girl like her on his side. "You know which one I am, right?"

She placed the second cup down as though it were as delicate as an eggshell, then stretched her hand out for a jar of instant coffee. She wrenched the lid off the jar, then yanked open a stubborn drawer, making the silverware clatter as she pawed around inside it.

He tried to will her to answer. He wanted to hear firsthand from someone who didn't share his last name, just what people in Mt. Knott thought of him and what he had done to his family's business. He wanted to hear it from *her.*

"I know which one you are." Her fingers curled around a spoon, and the room grew very quiet. Finally she said so softly that a draft from the nearby window might have blown the words away, "You're the man whose name is on my baby's birth certificate."

She did not look up. She went right on making the coffee. But it didn't escape Adam's attention that as she scooped the dark-brown powder into each cup, her hand trembled. With one sentence she shifted from a smart, sassy woman in control to one scared little lady.

That's just what he had wanted when he had first shown up tonight.

Then why didn't he feel better about it?

"What am I doing?" The spoon clinked against the inner lip of the cup. She shut her eyes and shook her head. "I should have heated the water first."

"Never mind." He straightened away from the cabinet.

"No. I'll fix this." She lifted both cups. They rattled against each other, tipping one and sending instant coffee spilling over the counter. "Now look what I've done, I—"

"Look, forget it." He stepped forward, feeling every inch the heel for having reduced her to this. "I don't need any coffee."

"No, I said I'd make it and there's one thing you ought to know about me, Mr. Burdett. If I say I'm going to do something, I do it." She set both cups down, then began to scoop up the dark dust in her palm. It sifted through her fingers like sand. "I can fix this. I can—"

"Josie." He took her by the wrist and turned her to face him. That's when he saw the tears rimming her eyes. They seemed held in place only by the sheer force of her will not to cry. He cupped her fisted hand in his palm. "I didn't come here for coffee."

"I know," she rasped. "You came here to take my son."

A few minutes ago he'd not only have agreed with her, he'd have thrown in a crude adjective to seal the deal. Now? All he could do was clear his throat and say, softly, "Then maybe we should just talk—"

She jerked her head up. "I'm not anything like my sister, you know."

He smiled then. "I can see that."

"You can?"

When she looked confused, Adam noticed, a small crease appeared between her eyebrows.

"How can you possibly see I'm not like Ophelia? We only just met."

"I can see it—" he rubbed one knuckle along her cheek as gently as he could manage "—because you're the one who's here with my son, not her."

"That's because…" Her voice failed. She blinked. A single tear dampened her cheek. She pushed out a shuddering breath. "I love him. He's mine."

It killed him to hear that, and at the same time it made him proud and elated to know his boy had been loved and wanted by somebody. Adam studied her with a series of brushing glances.

Not just *somebody,* he realized when his gaze searched hers. The baby's aunt. His birth mother's identical twin. Someone with a blood bond and a heart with the capacity to put her needs aside to care for a helpless infant.

And grit. Josie had to have grit, he decided on the spot. How else could a woman choose to bear the burden of single motherhood? How else could she stay in Mt. Knott and watch the jobs and opportunities ebb away, partly because of his own actions, and even begin her own business because she knew she had to provide the sole support for a child?

"You can say that? After Ophelia just dumped him on you?"

"I never said she—"

"But that's what she did, right?"

The woman lowered her gaze to the floor. "It doesn't change how I feel about him."

Adam swallowed, and it felt like forcing a boulder through a straw. Everything he'd determined about this lady flew right out the window when he considered all he'd learned in just a few moments with her. He liked her plenty, in all manner of ways, most he didn't even understand yet—and he reckoned she was plenty good for his boy, as well.

"Please, Mr. Burdett," she whispered, her chin angled up and her eyes bright with unshed tears. "Please tell me you haven't come to take away my baby."

"Actually, ma'am, I…" Adam sighed.

Who was he kidding? He couldn't take his son away from the only mother the baby had ever known. He wouldn't.

"I haven't come to take him away, Josie."

She shut her eyes and mouthed the words *thank you.*

Adam didn't know if she spoke to him or to heaven—maybe both. He took one step back. So he'd wimped out of doing what he'd come here to do. That didn't mean he'd called a complete surrender…and he respected this woman enough to make sure she understood that without question.

"But I think you should understand, ma'am." He stuck his thumb through his belt loop and anchored his boots wide on the gleaming vinyl floor. "I won't simply sign some papers and walk away, either. He's my boy and I'll do whatever it takes to make sure I stay involved in his life. *Whatever* it takes."

Joy and apprehension battled within Josie, and in the end joy won. He said he wasn't going to take her baby. Knowing that, she figured she could handle anything else thrown at her by this biker/cowboy with a voice that poured over her nerves like honey over sandpaper.

"Then let's talk, Mr. Burdett." She extended her hand toward the small kitchen table, her hope renewed that this could still work out in her favor. "If you still want some coffee, I can—"

The sputtered coughing cry of the baby halted her offer and Adam Burdett's movement toward the table at the same time.

He gave her a quick, panicked look. "That him?"

"Unless my cat's become a ventriloquist, I'd say yes." She laughed but couldn't make it sound real, not knowing that if the baby awakened she'd have to let this…this…*father* person see him. The very notion made her heart race.

She cocked her head to listen, praying that the baby was merely restless and would quiet and go back to sleep on his own.

"You got a cat?" Burdett leaned into the doorway to stare down the hall in the direction of the bedroom.

"What?" She blinked, moving to the door to lean out just a bit farther than he did.

"A cat." He slouched forward, his face a mask of concentration all focused on any sound that might arise from the child. "I heard it said that it's not good to have a cat around a baby."

"That's an old wives' tale." Josie rolled her eyes.

No other sound came from the baby's room. She relaxed enough to appreciate the level of confusion and worry on Burdett's face over the routine sounds the baby had just made and some silly superstition.

The baby was quiet. Maybe the fact that she'd dodged the letting-him-see-his-son-for-the-first-time bullet made her warm a little to the man. Or maybe it was the tenderness in those eyes that allowed her to loosen up a bit and say, "You don't know much about babies, do you, Mr. B— I mean, Adam?"

"This is my first," he said softly.

"Mine, too," she said, even softer.

She bet no other new parents had ever shared such an awkward or awkwardly sweet moment. Josie found within herself the power to actually smile. Maybe after a few meetings, a few long talks about parenting philosophy, visitation expectations, some practical lessons in the care and feeding of a one-year-old, she'd be ready to allow this man to see their son. Then later, maybe, after he'd proved himself capable, he could hold the baby and—

Just then the baby broke out in a howling lament.

Josie froze.

"I don't know much about babies, ma'am." Burdett glanced at her and then down the hallway, his whole body tense. "But I do know that means someone needs to go check on him."

She took off before he finished the sentence. Josie heard his big old boots clomping along the hallway right behind her stocking feet and it irritated her.

"So then, you're saying it's okay—your cat and the baby?"

"What cat?" She spun around, placing one hand and one shoulder to the bedroom door. He practically loomed over her as she glowered up at his concern-filled face and snapped, "I don't have a cat."

"You don't?"

"No."

The baby wailed again.

"But I do have a child who needs my attention. Now if you'll just go wait in the kitchen and excuse me, I'll take care of my baby." She started to slip inside the room without opening the door to any unnecessary invitation.

His arm shot past her head, his palm flattened to the door just inches from her eye level. "Whoa, there, sweetheart."

She twisted her head to peer over her shoulder.

"I promised I wouldn't take the baby from you." His dark eyes went almost completely black. She saw the heat in his cheeks and felt it on his breath as he lowered his voice to a raw-edged whisper. "But I double-dog promise you something else, as well, I won't take *this* from you, either."

"What?" A corkscrew curl snagged on her eyelash and bobbed up and down as she batted her eyes in feigned innocence.

"I won't take this game of trying to shut me out of my baby's life. I want to make that very clear."

It was. And despite the anxiety it unleashed in her, Josie realized, she respected and admired his attitude. For a year now she had painted the baby's father as some sleazy party animal who hadn't even cared enough to find out what had become of Ophelia. It gave her some curious comfort now to know that wasn't the case. Her son had a decent man as a father.

A decent, gorgeous, Harley-riding, Mt. Knott-deserting rich man who could change from rapt pre-occupation over his child and some imaginary cat to issuing hard-nosed mandates about the boy in a matter of seconds, she reminded herself.

"Do you understand that, Josie?"

She understood that and so much more. Like her problems with the diner and the simple existence she had known before she took in Nathan, from this point forward the life she had planned was going to take a different turn, and, like it or not, it was going to have to include Adam Burdett.

Chapter Three

They both shuffled quietly inside the room, using only the stream of light from the hallway to guide them.

"Hush, now, Nathan, shhh. Quiet down. It's all right." Josie, standing in profile to Adam, cooed some kind of magical, maternal comfort to the lumpy blue blanket she pulled from the crib.

"Nathan?" He turned the name over and over in his mind. He liked it. "Is what you named him?"

"Yes. It means…" She snagged her breath and held it a moment. "It's Biblical. It means gift."

"I like it." He found himself nodding slowly to show his approval.

"I'm glad," she whispered, but nothing in her body language underscored her claim. She cuddled the baby close and spread the blanket out over the two of them so that Adam could not even see a tiny finger or a lock of fine baby hair.

He longed to lay eyes on his boy for the first time, show himself and say, "Hello, Nathan. I'm your father. I'm here now. I won't allow you to grow up feeling as if the people who should have done anything within their power to keep you, gave you away and didn't care."

Adam knew most adopted children did not feel this way. But he had. He had been *made* to feel that way. And now that he had returned to Mt. Knott, he would not only shield his child from those emotions, Adam would make his remaining family pay for having treated him so callously. He had the means and the motivation. The news of his unexpected fatherhood had hastened his plan but had not quashed it. If anything, it gave him new passion for the battle that lay ahead. He would do this not just for the child he had been, but for the child lying in this small, dark room before him.

Adam strained to get a good look at the kid without getting too close. Deep in his gut, he truly wished to step forward and scoop his son up in his arms. But somehow his body would not cooperate. He hung back, his back stiff, his legs like lead, folding then unfolding his arms across his chest, then letting them dangle limp at his sides.

"Is he..." He craned his neck to peer around a tossed-back flap of the blanket that draped from Josie's shoulder to her midthigh. "Is he okay?"

"Well, he's not wet or...otherwise." She rocked

her body back and forth, and the crying died to gurgles and gasps.

"Maybe he's hungry." Just saying it made Adam feel all fatherly. Maybe this wasn't such a hard thing after all, to take care of a baby.

"I doubt that." She patted the bundle gently, still rocking.

"He would have had a bottle before bed."

"But babies eat at all hours." He spoke like a veritable authority on the subject even though, deep down, he felt like a complete dolt. Him! Adam Burdett, one of five highly valued and overpaid vice presidents of acquisitions and mergers for Wholesome Hearth Country Fresh Bakery, a division of Cynergetic GlobalCom Limited. How could one small, totally dependent creature reduce him to such uncertainty and ineptitude? "Don't they need to, um, refuel, during the night?"

"Refuel?" For the first time she laughed faintly.

But still, something in the sound of it made Adam long to hear it again.

"Yeah, you know. Like a minijet with diapers?" He pressed his lips together and made the sound of a sputtering engine. "Or a rechargeable battery."

"If they ever find a way to channel this kid's energy into a battery or an engine, I'll have to give up my job and chase him around full-time."

"Yeah, you wouldn't want that."

"Are you kidding? I'd love to give up worrying

about how I'm going to keep the Home Cookin' Kitchen open and be a full-time mom to Nathan." Her eyes grew wide suddenly. "Not that I want my business to fail. I love what I do. I love providing a service to Mt. Knott and seeing everyone, and I love cooking. Especially…well, my specialty is not important beyond, you know, being a mother being my specialty."

She was babbling. Not in a ridiculous, silly way. She was just nervous. And relieved. Nervous and relieved all at once. He could sense that in the way her words all ran together, then stopped suddenly. He didn't learn much from what she said, of course, but it did help him see her inner conflict over her roles as a woman business-owner and a mother to his son.

"But if I could somehow not have to keep the crazy hours at my Home Cookin' Kitchen and could just spend all my time with Nathan, at least in these early years, I'd do it in a heartbeat. No regrets. No complaints." She stopped abruptly again, and this time her eyes grew wide before she added, in a little slower and more pronounced voice, "Not that I'm hinting that's what I expect you to provide."

She'd babbled until she had spoken the truth. In doing so, she'd given Adam a glimpse into her desires and perhaps some future negotiating power. He filed the information away and, on the surface, let it go. "So, he's not hungry?"

"No. I don't think he's hungry." She kept swaying

back and forth and jiggling the baby, who had begun to fret and grunt quietly beneath the blanket. "He's been sleeping through the night for a couple of months now."

"He has?" Adam was rocking now, too. He couldn't seem to help himself. Though he wasn't sure, he figured this was how it felt to carry on a conversation on a boat. "Well, maybe he's sick, or needs some—"

"Maybe…" she interrupted in the same soothing murmur she used with the baby "…he just had a bad dream."

"Dream?" He stopped rocking long enough to consider that. "What on earth does an itty-bitty baby like that have to dream about?"

"He's not so itty-bitty. He's got plenty of things to dream about, a whole lifetime of experiences. *His* lifetime." She shot him a look that even in the dim light Adam interpreted as a challenge. *I have been this child's mother for his entire life. Where have you been?* "He'll have his first birthday in two weeks, won't you, tiger?"

"He will?" Adam stretched out his fingers, needing a kind of visual cue to help him do some lightning-fast math. "That means he was born in September, so August, July, June—"

"January."

"What?"

"He was conceived in January, one year, eight months and two weeks ago." She faced him, her mouth set in grim accusation. "Don't tell me that doesn't even ring a bell. Maybe you've just been with so many women that it's all a blur."

"Oh, it's a blur all right, but not for the reasons you think." He scratched at his cheek while his mind struggled to force all the pieces together. "Maybe you don't recall this, but…"

Adam faced a choice. Speak the truth and risk having it sound like a plea for pity or at least leniency for his behavior or skim over it. He could stand here and own up to that bad behavior without any preface or attempt to put it in context.

His mother had died. He felt he had not only lost the only one who'd seen him truly as her own but that he had also lost his place in his family. When his suggestions to take the Carolina Crumble Pattie to a wider market had been ridiculed by his father and brothers, Adam felt he had lost his reason for staying in Mt. Knott as well. By the time he met Ophelia, a beautiful woman who shared his disdain for the small town, he had not been thinking about right and wrong.

He had been in pain. He needed to feel he wasn't a lost cause, just a stray that nobody wanted. He felt worthless and figured he didn't matter to anyone, not even God. It became easier to fall into sin, he had learned, when you take your eyes off the Lord and start looking at the mess you have made of your life and the mess life has made of the world around you.

He had long prided himself on being a man who

told the truth. It was one of the things, he felt, which set him apart from his father.

While Conner Burdett was not a dishonest man, he had built his business on the belief that knowledge was power. And Conner protected his own power by controlling what knowledge he allowed others to have.

On the other hand, telling her about all the years of pain and loneliness that led up to those few wild nights that January would probably just sound like an excuse.

Adam didn't like people who made excuses. Besides, he had no way of knowing if he could trust Josie with an emotional truth that could cut him to his core. She may yet prove herself the enemy in a bitter custody case. He decided to tell the truth, but not all of it. It twisted low in his gut that he would follow his father's path but if she listened, really listened, she would hear the message beneath the words and have an inkling of what had fueled his angry rebellion.

"If you recall, I came into my inheritance in January." *I lost my mom. My only ally.*

Her determined jawline eased a bit.

"I found myself with a totally new status." *Finally, officially, on my own. Alone.*

Her gaze dipped downward.

"I didn't handle it particularly well." *I'm not making any excuses.*

She nodded, her brow furrowed. "I'm sorry about the loss of your mother."

"Thanks." He'd struck a chord, he supposed.

"She was a remarkable lady. A real force in the community. A good Christian who supported so many social causes and cared about people. She really put her faith in action."

"More than you probably know." He thought not only of how his mother had taken him in as a child and raised him as her very own, but also of the ways she devoted her own inherited fortune to help those in need. It tugged at Adam's heart to realize that back then he'd been so fixated on striking back at his father and brothers that he had done nothing to honor his mother and the things she had taught him. That did not alter his plan for revenge, however.

He was a Christian. He just wasn't *that* kind of Christian. He fought back a twinge of shame over having even thought that, much less allowed it to stand as his justification. "If it helps, I am not proud of what I did."

"I'm not the one you owe an apology to." Josie poked her chin up, fidgeted with the folds of the blanket that still concealed his son from him.

"An apology? I wasn't aware I owed an *apology* to anyone." It was what it *was*. He felt bad that it had gone so wrong. Felt some shame that his grief and resentment had uncovered his weaknesses instead of revealed his inner strength. But getting all touchy-feely about it now wouldn't change the past or set things right today.

He had come to town with only two indisputable responsibilities, to claim his son and ruin his so-called family. Neither Josie nor Ophelia Redmond figured prominently in his designs. "Your sister was a willing partner in what happened between us. Don't forget that she was the one who failed to notify me about the baby. It's not as if I haven't paid a price for my poor choices."

"I don't doubt that." She gave him a look of sympathy that did not sink to the level of pity.

He hadn't known anyone who had ever managed that with him and appreciated it in a way he could not for the world have articulated. His whole life, people had given with one hand and taken away with two. Encounters with even the most sincerely empathetic often left him undermined and exposed. He wondered if Josie would finally be the exception.

"However…"

"I should have known," he muttered under his breath.

"Hmm?" she asked over the wriggling and almost inaudible fussing of the baby in her arm.

"Give with one hand, take with two," was all he felt compelled to say.

"However…" She patted the blanket and adjusted the form beneath it, raising it higher against her own small frame. The legs kicked and a tiny hand flailed out to grab a strand of her hair. She ignored it and forged on. "Your *choices* have resulted in this small

life. And whether you have suffered enough or who is to blame for how the two of us arrived in this situation no longer matters. When you are a parent, it's not about you and your feelings anymore, it's about what's best for your child."

"My child," he echoed softly. "Thank you."

"You're welcome." She batted her eyes in a show of seeming disbelief, then leaned back to look under the blanket and the wriggling infant in her arms. "I don't usually yell at strangers like that, but…"

"I'm not thanking you for yelling at me." He chuckled at the very notion. He could go just about anywhere in this town and get yelled at, and by people a lot more experienced and colorful at it than Miss Josie Redmond.

"Then, I don't—" She hook her head.

"When," he explained as softly as the baby's gentle stirring.

"What?"

"You said *when* you are a parent. Not *if*. Your intention with that little speech was to put me in my place. And with that small distinction, you did." He reached out and brushed the blanket from atop the child's head.

The baby squirmed and made a sound that went something like "ya-ya-ya," then laughed.

Neither music nor birds nor even the grandest of majestic choirs could ever sound as sweet as the sound of his baby laughing.

"Anyway," he explained, knowing he'd have to appease Josie in some way before she'd even think of allowing him to hold his son, "I admit to my part, my shortcomings in all of this. I did spend time with your sister, obviously, and—"

"And it didn't mean a thing to you."

He lowered his head and his tone and took one step toward the woman holding his son. "You will never understand what it meant to me, lady."

She cupped the baby's head and took a step back from him. "Then why didn't you call her? Why didn't you try to find out what happened to her?"

"Because..." Again a choice loomed before him. Tell the whole truth and risk losing some of his power in the situation or say just enough to get what he wanted now. He looked long and deep into Josie's defiant yet anxious eyes and knew he only had one real course of action. The truth. "Because I was only thinking of myself. I acted like a wounded dog, snarling and mean and willing to do anything to protect myself. I spent a night with your sister, drunk most of the time but aware of what I was doing, and then I walked away and never looked back. Because that's what suited me."

There he'd said it. He'd given her plenty of ammunition to take a potshot at him and do some emotional damage. He did not deserve this child. But, as he hoped both his words and tone made quite clear, he would do whatever it took to be a part of young Nathan's life. *Because it suited him.*

"Oh." Clearly she did not know what to make of that. But she did not seem even remotely willing to use his confession against him. "Are you saying that if you had known sooner, you'd have returned sooner?"

"No." Again he spit the hard truth out. He had worked diligently this past year and a half to put himself in a position to do the most damage to…or good for, depending on one's vantage point, the Carolina Crumble Pattie Factory. If he had learned about his son sooner, he would have come for the child, but not until the time was right. "No, I can't say I'd have come back sooner. But I can say I am here now and that's what we have to deal with."

They stood in silence for a long, anxious moment.

Adam could practically see the thought process playing out over Josie's features. He wanted to say something to tip her confidence in his favor, but in the end he could only say straight-out what was on his mind. "You asked me earlier tonight not to take your son away, Josie, and I agreed. I won't. I can't do that to him—or to you."

He focused on her, standing in the shaft of light from the open door.

She seemed so small and alone in the otherwise dark room, that he felt drawn to her and the child cradled against her body.

He moved in, so near that he could see the fearful questioning in her eyes. He knew how it felt to wonder if anyone was on your side. To pray not to lose the person you loved most in the world and wonder how you would survive if the worst came to pass. He had prayed that prayer the night his mom died. But he had not come to destroy *this* little family. He had it within his power to prevent his son from losing the only mother he had ever known. He would not fail little Nathan in that regard.

Because, even though he had only known about him for a short while and had yet to even properly see him, Adam already loved the little guy. He supposed that among all his many faults and flaws, this redeemed him just a little. That in this feeling he knew a small taste of the greatest love of all, the love of God.

He placed one hand upon his baby's head and one protectively on Josie's tense shoulder. "Since you know I'm not going to take the boy, Josie. Why don't you just let me…hold him?"

She wet her lips. Hesitated.

"Please."

In one fluid movement Josie swept her hand beneath the child legs and then carefully laid him in his father's arms.

His son. Adam caught his breath. For all his good intentions and promises, holding his child for the very first time made him wonder if he'd spoken too soon. He did not want to tear this baby from the only mother it had ever known, but this was his son. His flesh and blood. And Adam would not settle for weekends and every other Christmas, just experiencing bits and pieces of his childhood.

He felt Josie tense at his side, but he didn't focus on her discomfort. Adam had always made his own rules in life—or figured a way around the ones he didn't like. That's exactly what he was going to do now.

He gazed into the baby's bright blue eyes and found just enough voice to whisper, "Hello, son. Daddy's here now. Daddy's here—and nothing is going to come between us ever again."

Chapter Four

"*Nothing's going to come between us again.*"

Adam's words to Nathan still rang in Josie's ears twelve hours later as she rushed about the diner trying to get ready for the morning coffee crowd.

Yes, *crowd.*

Large cities and fancy coffee shops and cafés with big noisy machines were not the only places that people liked to gather to chat on their way to work in the mornings. There had always been the usual fellows, the retirees who liked to do a little of what locals lovingly called, "pickin' and grinnin', laughin' and scratchin'." They met every day but Sunday, of course, to solve the problems of the world, tell jokes and stories they had all heard a hundred times, and reward their long-suffering wives with a little bit of "me" time.

Then there were the commuters. Ever since the layoffs had started at the Crumble, more and more folks began their drives to workplaces in other nearby towns with what Josie had listed on tent cards on the tabletops as "Cup O' Joe To Go." It wasn't the kind of thing you could get at those fancy places. No *grande* or *venti* size disposable cups with insulated wrappers to keep the drinker from burning his or her hands or fancy tops that looked like Nathan's sippy cup. No, this was a bank of coffeepots, sweetener options and creamers where people walked in, filled up the coffee conveyance brought from home, dropped a dollar or two in an old pickle jar and headed off to face the day.

Often stopping to share a word of encouragement with one another or to check the chalkboard for messages or new prayer requests. Always with a sense of community that one couldn't find anywhere else.

This was, to Josie, the essence of why she lived in Mt. Knott. It was also one of the reasons she had brought Nathan to work with her this morning. She felt safe here and felt her son would be safe here, as well.

Not that she thought Adam would do any harm to Nathan or even break his word about taking the child but…

But in her whole life she could not recall ever having felt so vulnerable.

A product, she suspected, of more than just Adam's introduction into Nathan's life. This emotion was also a byproduct of her realization that the man would be a presence in *her* life for a long time to come, as well.

She went up on tiptoe to peer over the cash register at the baby playing quietly in the bright blue portable playpen in the corner of the café.

She had promised herself she wouldn't make a habit of bringing Nathan to work. Maybe when he was older, she had thought, she would have him come by after school. He could do his homework in one of the booths and she would serve him a snack and whatever advice she could spare until he got into calculus or something else she knew nothing about. But until then she had determined she would have him at work as little as possible.

Josie didn't need to bring him here, really. She had been blessed with a network of moms and grandmothers around town who had taken turns watching her son since Ophelia left him in her care. The original plan was to depend on this patchwork safety net just until the newborn was old enough for day care. Well, that had been the plan, but then when the jobs began to dry up, so had the town's only day-care center.

She wondered if Adam Burdett would see that as unacceptable and use it as a wedge to take Nathan from her. He had promised he wouldn't do that, but then, what did she really know about him?

"Adam Burdett?" The first person she had asked, not giving the particulars behind her sudden interest in the man, had pondered it a moment. "Oh, Stray Dawg! Yeah. Yeah, I know which one he was, uh, is. The one who cashed out. Cut and run."

"Heard he went through that cash in nothing flat." The woman at the cash register took her change from Josie and, as she dropped the quarters and nickels into her coin purse, she elaborated, "Gambling." *Clink.* "Drinking." *Clink.* "Women." *Clink. Clink.*

"Gambling?" Josie shoved the cash drawer shut. "Drinking?"

"And women!" Warren and Jed confirmed in unison as they broke off from the morning gathering of curmudgeons to take their usual seats at the counter.

Of course Adam had women. A wealthy, handsome man like that probably had all kinds of girlfriends. She blushed at her own lack of sophistication and what many people would *tsk-tsk* as simple, out-of-date values. To hide her chagrin, she ducked back into the kitchen to check on the morning's first offering of pies still cooling on the racks beside the oven. *Girlfriends?* She doubted very much that a man like that thought of his conquests as girlfriends.

The aroma of apple and cinnamon and other spices filled the air. The tart sweetness of cherries bubbling in deep-red juices stung her nose. All buffered by the homey smell of flaky crust and Josie's specialty topping.

She went to the back door and cracked it open a tiny bit, to allow some fresh air into the hot, almost steamy kitchen. She paused only a moment, lifting her ponytail and turning her head to cool the back of her neck before hurrying back to her tasks, and to talk of Adam. She peered through the door and shut out the noise and views of the room around her.

"Ended up with a factory job, they say." A man took a wad of bills from his wallet, showed them to some fellow coffee-bar patrons as if to say "this one's on me" then stuffed them into the pickle jar. "Ironic, huh?"

"Reap what you sow." One of his cohorts raised his mug in grateful salute for the freebie. "Bible says."

Josie glanced around for one of the silicon gloves she used to handle hot pie plates and the like. When she didn't find it immediately, she grabbed the nearest dish towel and used it to cover her hand as she picked up one of the cherry pies. She didn't want to miss a word of the conversation in the dining room.

"I spotted that Adam at a hotel in Raleigh a year ago. Back when my husband went to that International Snack Cake Expo deal, remember?" spoke up Elvie Maloney, who had just started coming in after she went back to work when her husband lost his middle-management job at the Crumble. "Kept to the outskirts of the show. Didn't interact with the old gang, not at all."

"Well, can you blame him?" Micah Applebee scoffed. Micah had worked out at the Crumble for even longer than Elvie's husband. "After the mean-spirited way the Burdetts treated him?"

"The way they treated him was to make him a millionaire," Elvie shot back.

"Wish they'd up and treat me like that. I wouldn't even care if it was mean-spirited," Warren joked.

"You say that now but you'd come in here blubbering like a baby," Jed teased.

"Yeah, and using hundred-dollar bills to dry my tears," Warren said right back. They both laughed.

"Well, that Stray Dawg Burdett boy might have done better using money for hankies. It might have got it soggy but at least he'd have some of it left." Elvie whirled her spoon through her coffee.

"How do you know he doesn't?" Jed asked.

Elvie tapped the spoon on the edge of her cup, making everybody look her way. "Because he was at that conference working for somebody else. If I had millions, the last thing I'd want to do is work in a snack-cake factory all week and go to conferences on snack cakes on the weekend. Real suspicious if you ask me."

"Suspicious don't begin to tell it when you're talking about that one." A man wedging himself between two other people at the coffee bar snatched up a decaf pot and poured two cups worth into a thermal travel mug as he called out. "He's a wild one."

"The *smart* one, you mean," someone else at a nearby table chimed in. "Got out while the getting was good."

"Really?" Josie tried to fit the pieces of information together. That wasn't as easy as it seemed. While she sincerely wanted to believe the best of the man, she didn't dare allow herself to dismiss words like *suspicious, cut and run, gambling*...and *women*. As in multiples. *Many*.

The man who wanted to claim his place as her son's father had been up to something since he'd left town, and Josie needed to know what. And why he had come back, if it wasn't for Nathan's sake alone. She stole a peek at her boy and exhaled in relief to see him happily laughing over a game of peekaboo with Jed. She'd done the right thing by bringing Nathan with her today. She simply could not risk letting that wild one, that stray, that Adam Burdett get his hands on her son.

Not until she knew more about the man.

She set the pie down, wiped a blob of cherry filling on her starched white apron and asked, as she headed back toward the kitchen, "Is that when things soured at the factory? When Adam left?"

"Die was cast long before that." Jed paused with his red bandanna kerchief held up between him and Nathan.

"Oh?" Josie tried to sound as if she didn't care, but deep down it gave her some solace to know Adam hadn't been involved in the downward spiral of her beloved Mt. Knott. "I worked there for years, part-time most of it, but still, I never once saw any signs of the place heading for disaster."

"What's the Bible say? Pride goes before the fall? I reckon that place ran on pride, mostly, the last few years. When the mama died, that really tore things, though." Jed made a show of inhaling the scent of pie, sighed then jerked the kerchief back down and made a face at the baby, much to Nathan's delight. "Can't say how many times my wife came home after a quarterly meeting worried for her job. Hear her tell it, the son that took off was the only one bold enough to stand up to his daddy and say things had to change or they'd go under."

Josie's heart swelled a little at that. It warmed her to know her son's father had once shown true concern about the business that supported so much of her hometown.

She took up another pie, using only the dish towel as a hot pad and whirled around to peer into the front room from the kitchen. "So then, Adam Burdett is basically a good guy?"

"Yes he is," came the whispered response from behind her. "And I'd appreciate it if you didn't talk about me behind my back."

Splat.

"Awww." Came the collective groan from the patrons.

The damp smell of pie, apple this time, rose around her. The heat from a stray piece of fruit burned Josie's toe through her discount-store tennis shoe. Bits of crust lay smashed to smithereens all over the brown-red tile.

"Can you salvage any of it, honey?" either Jed or Warren asked.

She didn't try to distinguish between them as the other one quickly followed up with, "I had my mouth all set for a slice of that."

Josie walked farther back into the kitchen, shut out all the comments from her sympathetic customers and fixed her attention on the man who had slipped in through the open back door.

"I wasn't talking about you behind your back."

"No? Well, you sure were *listening* about me behind my back." He managed to sum up the situation without coming off arrogant or angry.

She smiled. "Then come on out in the open. I'm sure people here will be more than happy to talk about you right to your face."

He did not look amused.

Josie felt bad. She hadn't meant to hurt his feelings. She'd only tried to lighten the mood, to distract the man a bit after he'd caught her trying to find out more about him. And…and she wanted to show him her diner.

There. That was it. For some reason she wanted her baby's father to see what she had accomplished this last eight months since the first round of factory layoffs. She wanted him to know his son was being cared for by someone with drive, ambition, good sense and…and her very own pie carousel.

"I was just kidding, Ad—"

He put his index finger to his lips to cut her off. "Please. Don't say my name."

She glanced over her shoulder toward the dining room, which had gone uncharacteristically quiet. "Why not?"

"I don't want anyone to know I'm here. Not yet. I'm staying at a hotel on the highway and being very careful about the streets I take. Please don't undo all that now."

"I have to ask again, why not?"

He glanced toward the dinning room as well, then lowered his head and his voice. "Look, I just came by to see the kid. Went by your house and your neighbor told me you had to take him to work with you today."

Wanted to, not had to, she thought. To keep him safe from you. And she was wise to do it, apparently, since the man had already been by her home and it wasn't even 9:00 a.m. yet.

As if he sensed her trouble, the small boy in the playpen in the corner of the café shouted and threw a toy in the direction of his mother.

And on the heels of that, Jed, who had been playing with the child, stood up and called out, "Everything all right in there, Sweetie Pie?"

"Sweetie Pie?" Adam stood just inside the door of the kitchen.

Josie rolled her eyes then began pushing at the mess on the floor with the toe of her already pie-plopped shoe. "That's what everyone around here calls me."

"Oh?" Adam squatted down and used the pie pan to scoop up the mess. Unlike the spoiled, rich, suspicious-acting man she had been warned about, he didn't seem to mind getting his hands dirty. Josie could not say the same for his sense of humor. "I thought that your sister was more the everybody's sweetie type."

"Leave my sister out of this," she snapped.

He dropped the pie—pan and all—in the trash, then wiped his hands off on a towel.

Josie rushed over and snatched the pan out again. "I already lost the cost of ingredients on that. I can't afford the price of a perfectly good pan, as well."

"Sorry," he said, and seemed to actually mean it. "My mind was on other things… Sweetie Pie."

Josie heaved an exaggerated sigh, then went to the cherry pie that had been cooling all this time, cut a healthy slice, slapped it on a plate, then pressed that into his hand. "They call me that because of this."

He gave her a wary look.

"What's the matter? You too good to eat small-town-diner, homemade pie?"

"No one ever accused me of being too good for anything, ma'am." He dipped his head, his eyes glinting. "But my mama did manage to instill enough manners in me that I try not to eat pie with my fingers. At least not in front of a lady."

Josie blushed at her oversight and hurried to get him a fork.

He dug in, taking as big a bite as the fork would hold. He tasted. He paused. He swallowed. "Mmm."

"Does that mean you like it?" Why it was important for this man to like her pie, Josie didn't want to think about. But it was. Very important.

"So good it gives me an idea."

"I thought we'd already established I am nothing like my sister."

"Leave your sister out of this." He wagged his fork at her in warning.

She blushed again. Guilty of the same thing she had just nailed him over.

Jed called out, "Sweetie Pie? You having trouble with that clean-up in there?"

"No." Josie would not lie but she didn't want to just disregard Adam's request totally. "I'll be out in a minute."

"Thanks." He took another bite, set the plate aside and began looking around. "I don't want people to know I'm in town."

"How could you possibly keep a thing like that a secret?" Josie tugged up the corner of her apron to wipe his hands on. "Your father or brothers will be sure to make a big deal about your being back in town."

Using the hem of her offered apron, he pulled her close to him and dabbed a bit of pie filling and crust from the corner of his mouth.

The crisp cotton of her apron looked stark against the darker tone of his hands and face. Just as the whites of his eyes and teeth did. The contrast might have put her in mind of a wolf or some other predator, but when she let her gaze sink deeply into his eyes she felt just the opposite. She felt protected.

He let the apron drop.

Josie stepped away.

Adam put his hands in the back pockets of his black jeans and began looking around the kitchen as he said, "My father and brothers are the last people I want to know I'm here."

Josie did not have a suspicious nature but that did not sound good. She plunked her hand on her hip. "Well, forgive me for this, but…why?"

He said it along with her, his smile playful.

She folded her arms and did not laugh.

"I can't say, Josie." He took her by the upper arms as if he wanted to fix her in time and space so that his message could not go awry. "But I can tell you this—if people start talking about me, someone will remember I was with Ophelia."

"So?"

"So, then they will start putting the pieces together. They'll talk. Speculate. They buzz and carry tales back and forth, building them up, getting half the details wrong. That's the way it is in an anthill of a town this size, right?"

He was right about the nature of small towns, but he was wrong in assuming it was automatically a bad thing. "I heard it said once that a good neighbor is the best family some people ever have. That's how I feel about the people in this anthill. Outside of my grandmother and Nathan they are the only family I have. I don't plan to keep any secrets from them."

"Okay. I'm not asking you to keep secrets so much as to not volunteer anything for as long as possible. Not yet. To everything there is a season, right?"

Josie raised an eyebrow at his ease with scripture. She wondered if she should be impressed or insulted that he could pull it out so readily for his use.

"I'm not suggesting you never tell anyone that I'm Nathan's father. Just that when you do, the timing should be right."

"Right? Timing?" Josie shook her head. Her stomach churned. "That certainly sounds a lot like keeping secrets to me, Ad—" she shifted her eyes to the bustle that had resumed in the outer room "—uh, mister."

"Fine, then think how this sounds. How do you think Conner Burdett will react to the news that he has a grandson right under his nose? One living in a small house with a single mom who sometimes takes the kid to work with her?"

The churning in her stomach turned ice-cold. She wanted to run out into the dinning room, snatch up her child, take him home and hide. Instead she reined in her fears and asked, "He wouldn't…could he… challenge me for custody?'

"I don't know what he would do, but if he wanted to, he could. Especially with me not firmly established in the boy's life."

"No. No. Adam. Don't let that happen." Josie went to him and placed a hand on his chest. She had no business making such a forward move. Only it was not a move. It was an act of desperation. "Please."

He put his hand on hers and held her in place before him so that he could gaze directly into her eyes. "I won't, Josie. I will do everything in my power to protect you and Nathan and to keep you together, always."

"Always," she murmured. She had no reason to believe the man, but she did.

"Hey, Bingo!"

Josie's heart skipped, but it wasn't because of Adam's promise. Or his nearness.

At least, she told herself those weren't the reasons.

She'd just been startled. She had been in the kitchen so long she hadn't heard Bingo beeping for her to come out and collect her mail. Now he'd had to climb down off his scooter and come inside to deliver the mail.

Talk about reasons to get the anthill buzzing!

"You know everyone, Bingo," called out a woman Josie did not recognize—not Elvie or one of the commuters—which only drove home Adam's point about how quickly all sorts of folks would be talking about him…and Nathan…and Ophelia. "Maybe you can help us out here. Remember the second Burdett boy?"

"Huh? Oh, yeah. Yeah. The Stray Dawg!"

Adam flinched.

Josie hesitated only a moment before putting her hand on Adam's sleeve and giving a squeeze.

"What do you know about him?" the strange woman asked again.

"Who's asking?"

"Josie was…where is that girl?"

"I'm still in the kitchen." She nabbed the pie pan with one slice missing and headed for the door, leaving Adam to finish clearing away the crumbs of the pie she had dropped.

"Hey, Sweetie Pie." Bingo waved to her with the stack of mail in his hand. "Interesting y'all should bring up that Burdett now. Didn't your sister spend some time with that Stray Dawg last time she were in town, Josie?"

"I, uh…" Josie would not lie but she couldn't bring herself to jog the memories of people who might unknowingly threaten her relationship with Nathan.

"That's how I remember it." Bingo placed the mail down on the counter. "Not long after his mama's death. The pair of them tore around on that motorcycle of his, then they both up and disappeared."

"That's right," someone muttered.

"How could we forget that?" came another comment.

Bingo paused long enough to stretch his legs, being extra-careful of his bum knees. "Until that Ophelia came back to give Josie her baby…"

Grrr-eeee. It went so quiet in the room they could hear Bingo's joints creak.

Everyone in the room turned at once to look at Nathan.

Josie plopped the pie pan on the counter in front of Jed.

"Go get him," Adam whispered.

She did not need a second urging.

In a couple of steps she had the baby in her arms. "Oh, y'all, what imaginations."

Not a lie. Just an observation. *An observation intended to distract from the truth.* And it left Josie feeling guilty and uncomfortable.

"Now excuse me." She slipped into the kitchen without further explanation.

Adam met her with his hands open to accept Nathan.

Josie hesitated for a moment.

"You are going to have to trust me sometime, Josie. I am this baby's father and I am not going to just go away. If we hope to raise him together, we have to trust each other."

"To everything there is a season," she murmured back at him.

"Josie, hon? What's going on?" From the sound of Jed's voice, he had come around the counter and was headed for the door.

Adam looked at her.

"What will you do with him?" she asked.

"Take him to your house for now."

"You can't take him on your motorcycle!"

He smiled. "I'll walk. I can slip through the back alleys and side streets."

She pressed her lips together. She was about to let this man she had only just met, a man with the only claim to her son—until his father learned about the connection—just walk away with him.

"Sweetie Pie?"

What choice did she have?

"Go," she said. She gave her son a kiss on the temple, trying not to allow herself to imagine it might be the very last time she could ever do that. "I'll slip away and get home after lunch."

"We'll be there, Josie."

"I want to believe you," she said so softly that she knew the man retreating through the back door could not possibly have heard her.

Chapter Five

"Poor baby." Josie looked at her grinning son with his T-shirt on backward and inside out, only one sock on and wearing a cereal bowl on his head like a hat.

"Hey!" Adam, sitting on the floor in front of the couch beside the baby, fooled with the waistband of the clean but haphazard diaper, trying to get it to look right. He stood up and surveyed his work. "I think he's in pretty great shape considering I've never taken care of anything more demanding than my career or my Harley."

Nathan waved a wooden spoon like a regal scepter and babbled his favorite "ya-ya-ya."

"I didn't mean Nathan. I meant you." She laughed and trailed her gaze over the man.

Barefoot, baby powder smudged up and down his jeans, his once crisp business shirt had a row of tape—the kind Josie kept handy for when the disposable diapers came unstuck—down the front placard. His neck and the hollows of his cheeks were ruddy. The side of his hair that wasn't jutting straight up was globbed down by a blob of orange baby food.

"What?" He held his arms out.

"Nothing." She put her hand to the tip of her nose to hide her laughter, then added. "I like the new look. Takes business casual to a whole new level."

"Guess I could use a little…" He whisked the back of his hand down his jeans, creating a cloud of baby powder. Clearly pleased with that, he yanked the tape off, muttering, "Kid kept trying to eat the buttons, so I improvised a safety measure."

"Nice." She nodded. "And the reason for the mashed carrots in your hair?"

"The…" He thrust his fingers alongside his temple and raked them straight back. He winced. He withdrew his hand, stared at the orange goo there and exhaled in one exhausted groan. "I had no idea what I was getting into, obviously."

"You did fine, I'm sure." Better than Josie had suspected he would do. Her house was not in disarray. Her child was happy. "You hungry?"

"Am I ever." He reached down and picked up the baby, who promptly whapped him on the head with the wooden spoon. He didn't even miss a beat as he followed Josie from the room. "I didn't want to rummage around in your kitchen. But I did steal a taste of Nathan's baby food."

"You didn't!"

"I did." He made a face then backed up a few steps and slid Nathan into his high chair.

"How was it?"

"You know how some dishes—exotic food, delicacies, specialty dishes—a lot of times are better than they look?"

"Uh-huh."

"Well, baby food isn't one of those dishes." He worked his tongue around as if he was still trying to get the taste off. "When does he start eating real food?"

She laughed then bent to place a kiss on her son's cheek. "His diet is designed to help him grow healthy and strong."

"That's fine for him, but I'm already healthy and strong."

He certainly was. "Well, lucky for you I didn't take that into account when I made this plate up for you. I had taste in mind." She held up the "to go" box and flipped up the lid. The aroma of meat loaf and hot rolls and green beans and fried okra filled the room. The collection of some of her specialties was probably not the usual rich man's meal, but if the gossip proved true, Adam was no longer a rich man. Surely he'd appreciate the effort if not the flavor.

"Mmm. That smells wonderful." He took the container and inhaled deeply. "Fried okra? I love fried okra. My mom used to make that."

"Really?" Josie took a step, slid open a drawer and

retrieved a fork to hand him, all the time managing to keep the plastic grocery-style bag over her arm from swinging about and making a mess. "Did she ever make pie?"

"No, but she made cake—a few thousand a day."

Josie stilled. "Are you saying the Carolina Crumble Pattie was your mom's creation?"

"Yep. Well, it was an old family recipe that she perfected."

The idea her pies relied on an old Burdett family recipe improved upon by Adam's own mother warmed Josie all over. She opened her mouth to tell Adam so, but he stopped her by closing his eyes, lifting his chin, stretching up his whole body and taking a larger-than-life sniff of the air around them.

"I'll take care of Nathan for a week if you brought me a slice of pie."

"Then I guess you'll be taking care of him the rest of the summer and into the fall, because I brought you a whole pie." She let the bag rustle. "Sit. I'll get you a plate."

"Don't go to any trouble." He took a seat at the kitchen table. "This won't be the first meal I've eaten straight out of a take-out box."

"Nonsense." She grabbed a plate, then shut the cabinet door quickly so he wouldn't see that she only owned two decent place settings and one of them was chipped. "Food always tastes better when you eat it off a proper plate."

"Thanks." He transferred his lunch from the box, then grinned up at her when she put the whole browned-to-perfection pie to his left. "Must say, your pie certainly looks a lot better on a plate than on the floor."

"It's not the only thing that takes on a different appearance when viewed in a more welcoming context."

"Welcoming." He said it slowly, his gaze fixed in the distance. He waited a moment and she wondered if he expected to hear an echo or something. Finally he pulled his chair up close to the table and said, "I like that word."

"I mean it."

"I believe you do."

"And you don't believe your family would feel the same way toward you?"

"If they are smart they won't."

Josie didn't know what to make of that. Was his sentiment sad or sinister?

He dug in, unselfconsciously humming his approval with every bite.

Sad, she decided, and set about trying to change his perception. If you scratched the surface of his stoic, stone-faced, wounded-stray image, many things about Adam were just plain sad. "It all reminds me of the story of the prodigal son."

"No, Josie." He stabbed a bite of meat loaf. "This is nothing like that."

"It certainly seems—"

"No. The prodigal son came crawling back,

willing to live as a servant or to eat with the animals."
He gestured with the meat loaf still on his fork. "That
is not the case with me. No."

"Adam…"

"I've returned to Mt. Knott with a plan, and
humbling myself before my father is not part of it."
He took the bite, chewed, then struggled to swallow.

Josie couldn't decide if the food or the feelings
were responsible for that. Just in case, she jumped up
and got the gallon of milk from the fridge, poured
him a big glass, then plunked it down in front of
him. "If you don't hope to reconcile with your family,
then just why did you come to Mt. Knott?"

He froze with the glass of milk halfway between
the plate and his mouth. He shifted his eyes quite
pointedly in Nathan's direction.

"Don't give me some noble story about coming
for your son." She beat him to the punch.

By the look on his face he didn't know whether
to respond with indignation or by being impressed.

"If all you wanted was to claim Nathan, then you
could have sent a lawyer or the sheriff or, more logi-
cally, shown up on my doorstep with both of those."
That's how she'd envisioned it happening when she
had nightmares about it. "You needn't have bothered ruffling your hair with a long, nighttime Harley
ride for that."

"I would do far more than inconvenience myself
for my son." He touched his hair where the orange

baby food had been. "But I would never send a stranger to take him from his mother."

"His mother," she murmured.

No matter how many times she heard it from his lips, it still took her breath away. Ophelia had signed the proper papers and this man saw her, *Josie*—not her sister—as Nathan's mother. The thought of it caused a rush of hope to flood her being and she said a quick prayer that the Lord would bring to pass legally what she and Adam knew in their hearts to be true.

Then she went back on the defensive. Where her son was concerned, she could not afford to let down her guard for anyone. And she had to make sure Adam knew that, knew just what kind of person he was dealing with. "I'm saying I may not be one of those worldly, sophisticated women you are accustomed to—"

"What women?" he asked around a mouthful of okra.

She did not stop to answer his question, but just plowed right on with her thought. "But don't make the mistake of thinking I'm so naive I can't understand what's going on."

"I can assure you, I don't think of you that way at all." Another swig of milk. His dark brows angled down, he leaned forward on his elbow. "That said, I just have to ask—what *is* going on, Josie?"

"I have no idea," she admitted freely. "There. Now you know exactly who you are dealing with. A lunatic."

He laughed, then helped himself to a thick slab of pie.

She conceded her humility with a soft chuckle, then she sat back in the chair. "But you've told me this trip home, the timing, your plans are not just about Nathan. If not specifically, then by the things you *don't* say and the way you say them."

He set his fork down and allowed what she had just said to sink in.

He made her nervous. "See? A lunatic. But not one that's entirely off base on this. I know things are not what they seem on the surface. And I know that I would be foolish not to be wary about that. I also know that—"

"What *I* know is this is very good pie."

"Don't change the subject," she warned, then watched him stuff down a whopping bite, she went all mushy inside and had to ask, "Do you really think so?"

"I do." He laughed over her response and took another bite. "I've certainly tasted a lot of pastry products in my lifetime. Desserts and more than one person's share of snack foods, but this...this is special. Old family recipe?"

"I don't even have an old family." She shook her head and hoped that hadn't come off too pathetic. To try to counteract that, she scooted her seat in close and decided to share what she had discovered today, "I've got a secret ingredient that comes from an old family recipe, though."

"I bet you have a lot of secrets, Josie."

"No." She sat back. "I'm pretty much an open book."

"And me without my library card." He touched her hand.

She blushed. "My grandmother taught me how to cook. I lived with her from the time I…"

Became a Christian. She wasn't embarrassed to talk about her faith, but she didn't know any way of doing that without bringing up how her mother and sister had rejected her. And in doing so remind him that she was not Nathan's mother by birth. She wondered if that was a weakness of faith on her part? "From the time I moved to Mt. Knott in high school until she died a few years later, when I already had a job at the Crumble."

"You worked at my family's factory?"

"I told you that. Didn't I tell you that?"

Neither of them seemed to recall. That should have sent up a red flag to Josie that either the man wasn't listening to her or she wasn't paying attention to what all she said to him. Or perhaps that when they were together they were too…sidetracked to bother with the small details of a conversation.

She stared at her hands, determined not to look into his eyes in hopes she would remember this exchange in detail. "I didn't survive the first round of job cuts."

"I'm sorry."

"Thanks. But in a way it was a good thing. It put me in motion to open the diner."

"Yeah. Sure. What seems like a disaster can often provide people with the push they need to take control of matters, to make bold moves, to better their lives." He sounded as if he needed convincing.

Josie found this odd as he hadn't been a part of the mess at his family's factory.

"I had Nathan to support after all."

"You must have been terrified."

"Not really. I had my faith."

"In yourself?"

"In God."

"I can't…that is, I wish…"

"Your mother was such a strong woman of faith. Your brother has a wonderful, growing ministry. Don't you share their beliefs?" There. She asked it outright. She had to. The man was not just Nathan's father, it seemed that he was a seeker.

"It's not my mother, it's that…well, God is portrayed as a loving father, isn't He?"

"Yes."

"I don't know how to relate to that."

"Was your father really that bad?" Conner Burdett had always scared her. A powerful man, he tended to storm about not speaking, especially to an insignificant worker like her.

"Bad?" He cocked his head to the right and chewed slowly. "Wrong word."

"What's the right word?"

"Hard," he said quietly.

"He was hard on you?"

"He was hard on everybody, including himself, I think."

"Your mom balanced that out for him some."

"Yes, she did."

"But that didn't make him any less hard, I suppose."

"Hard?" He shook his head. "Maybe that's not it, either. Because, as you say, my mother had some influence over that. And he wasn't hard on any one person. There was a kind of fairness to it all. I think maybe the word I should have used is…unyielding."

"That is different. Subtly, but…"

"Like your secret ingredient, it can change everything."

She nodded. "I appreciate your being so honest with me."

"Don't kid yourself, Josie. Just because we've shared these few moments, you don't really know me. You don't really know what made me who I am."

"Who are you?"

"Haven't you heard? I'm the Stray Dawg."

"But if you have a hundred sheep and you lose one, that's the one that's on your mind. That's the one you worry about and go out and seek so that you can bring him home."

"You had Sunday school with Miss Minerva, too?"

"No. I told you, I didn't grow up here. I never had a home or a family or a regular church where I went to Sunday school each week. But I've always had a

Bible. And last night I looked up Luke 15, the story of the prodigal son."

Adam pushed his plate away, his mouth set in a grim line. "Maybe I made a mistake. Coming here, coming to you first before…"

"Before what?"

He did not look as if he felt any inclination to answer her, just took another bite of pie and stared at Nathan.

"Before what, Adam? What is it that you came to Mt. Knott to do?"

Even if he had decided to tell her, which Josie doubted very much, he did not get the chance.

A thunderous pounding on the front door made her jump. "Hello?"

She looked at Adam. Her heartbeat had gone completely awry. "Is that…"

"I guess we didn't get out of the diner fast enough to outrun the speculation."

"What are we going to do?"

Adam pushed away from the table, stood and reached for Nathan. "I am going to keep my son out of sight and you are going to go and get rid of my father."

Chapter Six

Adam stood behind the door of the bathroom, holding Nathan in his arms. In the split second he'd had to duck out of sight, it just seemed more prudent to do this rather than head to the door at the end of the hall. Josie's bedroom.

Yeah, Nathan's crib waited in that room, but so did every private thing about Josie. Her clothes. The pillow where she rested her head at night. The picture of her and Ophelia.

Adam had enough problems dealing with her without confronting those kinds of things right now. Besides, the bathroom was closer to the front door. Better situated to hear what Conner Burdett had to say.

"Hello?" the masculine voice boomed. The knocking did not relent. "Hello in there."

"Just a…" Josie put her finger to her lips to remind

him to stay quiet, then waved her hand to order Adam to close the door. "Just a moment, please."

"I know you're in there, young lady. Don't think you can hide from me."

"Hide? Me? Hide from…him?" Adam looked his son in the eye. "This is *not* hiding."

"Ya-ya-ya."

"No, really. That is *not* who I am. It's important to me that you know that, kid. I'm not hiding. I'm exercising discretion. Control. Got that?"

"Ya-ya-ya." Nathan waggled his head, his dark hair floating back and forth like down.

"Don't buy that, huh?" What Adam had intended as a joke left him uncomfortable and defensive. He met his own eyes in the bathroom mirror and frowned. "How about this? I'm protecting your mother. *Both* of your mothers."

"Hello?" Josie's voice was steady but tentative as the front door creaked open. "May I, um, may I help you?"

"Josephine Redmond?" Conner got right to the point.

The door creaked even louder.

Adam could imagine his father blustering in past Josie as if she wasn't even there. He clenched his jaw.

"Yes." Hesitation and anxiety colored Josie's usually warm, friendly tone.

"Good." Heavy footsteps thudded farther into the front room.

"Mr. Burdett, I didn't expect anyone to drop by today. Sir, if you don't mind..." She let her voice trail off, leaving her uninvited visitor to do what anyone with even the most basic good manners would do—apologize and offer to return when it was convenient.

Poor naive Josie. She must not have known that not only did Conner not mind that he'd inconvenienced her, he had counted on doing just that.

Keep 'em off balance. Always maintain the upper hand. Hold business meetings in your own office and if you can't, then never take a seat before your adversary. Conner had whole lists of edicts about interacting with others.

Adam had once asked, "What about people who are not your adversaries?"

"There are no such creatures, boy," Conner had replied with a look bent on driving home the point that the man included his own sons in that sweeping generalization.

"You didn't expect company," Conner's voice grew louder, a sure indication he had barged right into the house and had headed straight for the kitchen. "Yet here you just happened to bring a pie home from your restaurant in the middle of the day?"

Adam tensed. The last time he had heard that tone, that cadence of speech, that calculating manner, was the day he'd gotten a check, the lump-sum payment to buy him out of his share of the family business and the money his mother had left him in her will. He thought the next time he heard it, the man would be begging him to save the business. Now to hear him toying with Josie like this…

Adam flexed one hand over the doorknob. He wanted to go out there to rescue Josie.

Nathan squirmed.

He studied his son's face. Despite having only recently become aware the child existed, much less knowing him, just looking at him filled Adam with so much emotion. And he knew he would do anything to keep him safe. He knew Josie would feel the same way.

"Is that your way of asking for a piece of pie, sir?"

Silence. Conner hadn't seen that coming.

He wouldn't. Kindness and hospitality were foreign concepts to the old man.

"Good for you, Josie," Adam whispered.

"Uh, uh-huh. Pie would be nice." The tone shifted slightly. "Thank you."

Adam didn't know what to make of it.

"But what I'd rather have—" the old bluster returned "—is to get my hands on my grandson."

"Get your hands on?" Josie repeated the demand with hushed anxiety.

Adam hated this. Hated having to stand by and make her endure his father. He should be the one facing the old man down, bearing the brunt of the old man's belligerence.

"Just to hold him for a moment, you understand."

It was the quietest, most humble sentence Adam believed he'd ever heard his father speak to anybody but Maggie Burdett. Where did that come from? Who was this person standing in Josie's kitchen insisting…no, merely asking in humility and faltering hope…to see his only grandchild?"

"Where is the little fellow?"

"I…I don't think I should tell you that, sir."

Something between a wheeze and a chuckle answered her. "You've already told me more than you realize."

And just that fast the man Adam readily recognized as Conner Burdett resurfaced. He'd been a fool to think the seasoned bully could have changed. It had all been an act. An act to manipulate Josie and unearth answers.

"I haven't told you anything," Josie said.

"Oh, yes you have. For starters you didn't deny he was my grandson. Nor did you say you didn't know where he is, just that you didn't think you should tell *me*."

Adam drew in his breath and held it until his lungs ached. The Burdett offensive has just begun. Conner would go after Josie, hammer away at her with every tool in his considerable arsenal until he'd gotten every bit of information from her and left her in tears and fearing for her son's future.

"I know you have my flesh and blood." The words

came slowly, though Adam did not know if that was for effect or because Conner was choosing them so carefully. Either way they made the bile rise in Adam's throat. "The child is a Burdett and I have rights."

"Please, Mr. Burdett…" Josie's voice disappeared into a sob.

That was it. Adam could no longer stay out of this.

"This is my family, the son of my son," Conner boomed.

"Wrong." Adam stepped fully from the bathroom and reached the kitchen in just a few steps. "This child is *my* son. That makes him nothing to you but the child of some stray you took in and never really loved as your own."

You can know a man a lifetime and still not know everything that he is capable of, good and bad. That is not the kind of thing you can gauge in a matter of a few seconds. Unfortunately, sometimes a few seconds is all you have—so make them count.

Conner had taught Adam that a long time ago. Start with the details and work your way out. Listen to what a man tells you, but don't dismiss what your own gut has to say. Adam applied those skills now to quickly size up the old man.

Eighteen months ago, Conner Burdett made an imposing figure. Though in his sixties, the tall, raw-boned man had still sported a full head of mostly brown hair, keen eyes that sparked with grit and vigor and the ever-present authority that came from knowing no matter what, he still owned fifty-four percent interest in the family business.

As far as Adam could see today, that controlling interest in the company was all he still possessed. He made a fleeting study of the man before him.

The elder Burdett had lost weight. His hair had faded to white and thinned considerably. The newly developed stoop of Conner's shoulders had taken inches from his height. The man who had once seemed a veritable pillar of confidence to a younger Adam now stood almost eye-to-eye with him. And in those eyes Adam saw a weariness and remorse that had never been there before.

Adam clenched his jaw and reminded himself to listen to his own feelings. His son's future could well be at stake and he wouldn't risk it to something as deceptive as appearances or sentimentality. Conner Burdett was still capable of anything. *Anything.*

Adam braced himself to bear the full brunt of his father's wrath.

"Adam? Son?" Conner reached out. His hand shook. He took one step forward and then another as if he couldn't quite believe what he saw before him.

"Yeah?" Adam shifted his weight, pulling Nathan more to one side so that he could hand him off to Josie if he should need to.

"Thank you," Conner whispered and it was clear he meant it as heartfelt gratitude to God.

That humbled Adam but did not reassure him.

Then Conner placed his hand on Adam's sleeve, balled the fabric in his fist then pulled both Adam and Nathan into a tight embrace. "My prayers are answered. You've come home."

Adam stiffened.

Come home? Is that what he had done? He sought Josie. When their eyes met, he tried in one look to convey his confusion, his uncertainty, his panic.

She smiled. A wonderful smile that spoke of long longed-for reunions, at the joy of homecoming, of hope.

Conner took a deep breath and exhaled in short huffs as if he were...*sobbing?*

Adam tried to swallow. He had no idea how to respond to this. Anger, bitterness, rejection, even hatred—he had steeled himself well for any of those. But *this?*

"I, uh, I don't—" He started to pat the old man's back but couldn't bring himself to do it. Again he fixed his eyes on Josie's.

"You know what, Mr. Burdett? Why don't you come into the kitchen and have a seat while I dish you up a big old slice of that pie I promised?"

Adam had charged out ready to come to Josie's defense no matter what it took and here she had ended up rescuing him. And with nothing more substantial or less significant than pie.

"Hmm?" Conner pulled away at last.

"Pie?" She laid her delicate hand on the curve of

his shoulder to draw his attention toward her. "It's cherry. And if you'll have a seat, I'd be honored to serve you up a piece."

"Thank you, my dear." He gave her a nod. "But first, give me a moment. I want to…" He raised his hand.

Without thinking, Adam shied away, caught himself and forced his body to go perfectly still.

Conner's dry, trembling palm brushed along the side of Adam's face.

"I just…" Conner touched Adam's cheek, his jaw, then dropped his hand to his shoulder. "I just want to look at my boy."

My boy? Even commanding up every ounce of anger and disappointment he had ever felt toward this man, Adam could not make those words sound pejorative or hard-hearted. There was just so much yearning in them, so much peace and pride.

Don't you mean your stray? Adam wanted to say. Yes, wanted to say it with all his being. Not because it seemed appropriate but because he wanted to push the old man away.

He wanted to throw a barrier up between them. One that had existed there for so long. Adam had based his every decision the last eighteen months on the belief that that barrier justified his contemptible plan. And now…

And now Conner Burdett was standing before him, a shell of his former self, wiping a tear from under his eye with one gnarled knuckle. "I didn't

think I'd ever see you again, Adam. Not before…
well, not before we met again in heaven."

"Oh." The softest, saddest sound ever escaped
Josie's lips.

Adam looked at her, knowing she was thinking
not just about him and his father but also about what
she would have given to have heard such conciliatory
words from her own mother or even her sister. The
sweetness of her sorrow penetrated Adam's life-
hardened exterior and opened something up in him
that had been closed off for far too long.

"And this little fellow." Conner gave Nathan's
plump leg a shake. "Hey! I know who you are. Do
you know who I am?"

"Ya-ya-ya."

"Um, uh…" Adam had no idea what to say.

Conner didn't wait for him to come up with something. He lifted Nathan's small body from the crook
of Adam's arm. "You know who I am, little man? I
am *your* daddy's daddy."

"Since when?" Adam muttered, needing to put
things back in perspective. He stepped forward to
take the child away.

"Since the first time I held you in my arms. You
were about the same age as this young fellow."
Conner patted the small boy's belly. "Looked a lot
like him, except you were a skinny thing, with big,
sad eyes, and your hands always in tight little fists."

Adam froze.

Josie's gaze dropped from his face to his side.

He shook his hand to release the tension as he unfisted his fingers.

"And I felt about your daddy the way I bet he feels about you," Conner said to the baby.

Adam straightened, ready to deny that.

"That even though you two just met and the way things are in life, you may never really feel as though you are much more than strangers with a shared history, he would walk through fire for you." Conner did not look at Adam.

Which was a relief because Adam could not have looked at Conner then if his life depended on it.

Had he heard right? His father acknowledged that they were virtual strangers and yet he would walk through fire for him?

Walk through fire but not walk into a bar or cheap hotel in Mt. Knott in those days when Adam needed him to come and ask him to return to the fold. To say one-tenth of the handful of healing words he'd just uttered and pave the way for Stray Dawg to find his way home while it still meant something.

He couldn't accept that. Would not accept it. It was just talk, after all, from a man who made his living negotiating to get the better end of every deal.

Adam pushed his shoulders back. Conner wanted something. Adam could not be fool enough to let that slip from sight because the suddenly frail man had tugged at a few heartstrings.

"Why don't we sit down and have that pie?" Adam pulled Nathan from Conner's grasp, then went into the kitchen, settled the child in the high chair and pointed out a seat at the small oak table for Conner.

Josie frowned. Clearly she had expected more from Adam. Expected compassion, gratitude and mercy. Well, if that's what she thought she'd find in him, she had better get used to being disappointed.

But if, as Conner had put it, she expected nothing less of him than that he would walk through fire for her and their son, then he would never let her down. "Once you taste Josie's pie and spend a few minutes around Nathan you'll find yourself as proud as I am that she is the one raising my son."

Josie stilled with a knife posed over the pie. She blinked a few times and sniffled.

He tipped his head to her, affirming that was, indeed, how he felt. He hoped she knew, too, that he had just laid down the gauntlet. He had asserted his position and confirmed hers. He would brook no interference, no custody battle, no questioning of his decision from his powerful father or family.

She smiled and lifted her chin, making her soft, lovely ponytail bounce against her back. Then with a sidelong glance at Conner to make sure he wasn't watching, she served Adam the larger slice of the two pieces of pie.

He winked to show his thanks, then as soon as she set the plates down before the two men, he pulled the old switcheroo. Slid the larger slice right under Conner's nose and accepted the smaller portion for himself.

"You're going to want to have as much of this pie as you can hold," he told the old man, then leaned back and muttered to Josie, "and if his mouth is full it will give us more time to do the talking."

"Can I get you anything else? Some milk to drink? If you'd like some coffee you'll have to wait a minute while I brew up a fresh pot."

Adam thought of how she had told him to make his own instant the night he had come to claim his son and so he took her offer to make a pot for them as a compliment. Pie. Coffee. Kid. That should mollify the old guy just fine.

They'd show him what a fine home environment Nathan had. They'd get his assurance, for what it was worth, that he would not try to override their judgments about what was best for Nathan. They would send him on his way.

Then Adam's real work would begin.

Josie pulled a foil bag of coffee beans from a canister on the counter. The whir of her grinding them in a small electric appliance made it impossible to carry on a conversation for a minute or so. That, coupled with the time Conner was devoting to savoring his first bite of pie, gave Adam time to think things through.

He'd have to act fast. Make his move before the rest of the family found out how long he'd been in town without telling anyone. That fact would arouse suspicions. He loved his brothers but he would never make the mistake of underestimating them. Conner might have loved them more, but he certainly had not gone easier on them.

Burke, older than Adam by four years and known by all as Top Dawg, would be the first one to start putting the clues together. A few phone calls to contacts in the business would tell him plenty—*contacts, not friends.* Top Dawg had many things in life, money, looks, power, brains and the fawning adoration of most of the town of Mt. Knott, but the one thing he did not have was friends. Jason and Cody would neither know nor care about what Adam had in mind. They had long ago given up looking upon the lowly Carolina Crumble Pattie as their livelihood. According to Adam's sources, they each still held their small percentage of the company stock but did little else except show up for meetings and rubber stamp whatever Burke and Conner asked for. They would be no problem.

That left Conner.

The aroma of freshly ground coffee beans filled the air and Adam fixed his attention on the man sitting to his right. "Great pie, isn't it?"

"Very good." Conner jabbed his fork toward the half-eaten slab of golden crust and red, juicy cherries dripping in a thick syrup. "You know we could use something like this down at the Crumble. Your brothers keep telling me we need to try new things. Expand the line. Innovate. Burke says we have to do something or—"

"I'm glad you like it, sir." Josie finished loading the coffeemaker and pressed a button to start the brewing. It gurgled and grumbled and she turned her back on it to let it do its work. "But I don't think it would do you much good as a new product because I used—"

"Because she used to work for you already and you fired her. She has moved on." Adam lifted a bite of pie up as if offering a toast before he poked it in his mouth.

Josie gulped in some air. Her eyes got big. The room grew so quiet they could hear the coffee drip, drip, drip into the carafe. She shook her head. "Mr. Burdett, that's Adam talking, not me. I never said—"

"I'm sorry about your job, Ms. Redmond. We did what we had to do. Greater good and all. Been a regular struggle to keep the doors open these past few years, even though I haven't taken a cent out of the company myself, sunk everything right back in hopes of…not that it's made a difference."

Adam frowned. Had his father just apologized? And admitted weakness? And said he hadn't taken any money out of the company for *how* long?

"I absolutely do understand, Mr. Burdett. I am trying to keep my business afloat, as well." She poured a cup of coffee for Conner. Only Conner.

"Our layoffs can't have made that easier."

"No, sir." She pushed the sugar shaker and a bowl of creamer packets toward him. Still offering nothing to Adam.

"But that's going to change." Conner dumped two teaspoons of sugar into the rich dark liquid in his cup.

"It is?" Josie stood up, still not making a move to get anything for Adam to drink.

Frustrated, Adam considered getting up to fetch his own coffee, then decided to wait it out, and defiantly broke off a big piece of pie crust and ate it.

"Of course," Conner took a sip then beamed a huge smile. "Adam is back. Things are going to turn around now."

Adam coughed and covered his mouth to keep pie crust crumbs from spewing everywhere.

Conner forged ahead without the slightest response to Adam's reaction. "And to celebrate we're going to host a barbecue and invite the whole town."

"Oh, Mr. Burdett, I think that's exactly what Mt. Knott needs." Josie knelt down by Conner's chair, her whole face transformed with delight.

"Good. Then you can make the pies and, uh, side dishes, at your usual prices, of course."

Adam struggled to force down the dry bits of crust but it wouldn't cooperate. His fist came down on the table but not hard enough to bring a halt to the conversation. And this conversation needed to halt. His father had it all wrong. Adam had his own plans and he wouldn't let anyone or anything interfere with them.

"Mr. Burdett, you may have just provided me with a way to keep my doors open at least a little while longer!"

Adam gulped. He wouldn't let anyone or anything interfere with his plans, except Josie.

He had thought just moments ago that if she wanted him to walk through fire for her, he would never let her down.

He was about to prove that. Obviously he was about to walk through fire for her—and that fire would be in the form of a barbecue with his family.

Chapter Seven

Conner Burdett had gobbled up the last of his pie after he had offered Nathan a small taste, which the child smeared on his ear, his chin, his eyebrow, everywhere but his mouth. When Josie had come back from cleaning the child up, Conner had gone.

"He wanted me to give you this." Adam offered her a business card held between two fingers, the way she'd seen boys fling playing cards into hats.

She took if from him and, reading the words imprinted on it, understood why the stray Burdett brother might have wanted to send the card sailing as far away as possible.

"Burke Burdett," she read the name softly, scanned his official title and then studied the number handwritten beneath it. His private line. Not the kind of thing the average citizen of Mt. Knott was privy to. Josie turned the card over in her hand. On the back were the words, "Timetable. Menu. Payment" in shaky handwriting.

"I guess I'm supposed to call your brother about these things?"

Adam only nodded before he slipped Nathan from Josie's hold and turned the child so they could look each other in the eye. Of course, Nathan did not cooperate fully with that eye-to-eye plan, which made the picture of the father and son all the more endearing.

Adam sniffed the air. "One of us doesn't smell so good, buddy. Now, I'm always fresh as a mountain meadow myself, so I suspect it's *you.*"

Nathan giggled.

"I'll handle diaper duty, Adam."

"No. I can do it. I've gotten pretty good at it over the course of the day." He actually sounded pleased with his newly acquired skill. "Let's go, kid."

He draped the baby over one arm. The position made it look like Nathan was flying through the air, and loving it from the pleasant sounds he was making.

Good for Adam to get a little taste of what his own parents must have gone through with a headstrong, handful of energy in an adorable package. Looking at the two of them together now, she couldn't deny that Adam not only was Nathan's father but that he belonged in her son's life.

Her two fellas disappeared into the back room. Adam entertained the baby, alternating between making funny sounds and acting properly disgusted with the task at hand.

Josie leaned against the doorway and slid the card into her T-shirt pocket, knowing she'd forget where she'd put it if she put it in her jeans, and it would probably get washed with her aprons and other work clothes this evening. Then she stood back and waited for Adam to finish with Nathan. That first night she hadn't even wanted him to see the boy, now he was doing the dad thing as if he'd done it all along.

She couldn't help thinking of her own family. Not of the family made up of her mother and Ophelia, but the one she had always dreamed she would make for herself.

When she was a young girl, being hauled from town to town as her mother chased everything from dreams to men, that family meant a mom and dad, Ophelia and Josie. Also a baby brother or sister, or maybe a calico cat with a bell on its collar.

During her early years of living in Mt. Knott, when her grandmother was alive, she had been content to think of the two of them as their own special little family. Lately, though, being a single mother and running a business on her own sometimes had her daydreaming about what it would be like to have a husband as a helpmate. Not just to shoulder the chores and responsibilities but also to hold her hand in church and take her in his arms while they sat on the porch on warm summer evenings.

"Well, you may want to call in the toxic-waste disposal team to take care of that *diaper,* but I can sound the all's clear for the kid." He moved Nathan on his arm down the hallway again making a siren-type *waaa-ooo, waaa-ooo* before he reached the kitchen and said, "The kitchen is now safe for noses everywhere!"

She gazed at Adam holding Nathan. It was too soon to allow herself to wonder about Adam as potential husband material. In fact, his history with Ophelia made that prospect a bit…strained. Then again, when had anything with her sister been anything *but* strained?

That thought only made Josie feel more isolated. More adrift in the world. More wistful for her own home, family and husband, one who shared her values and would not disappear on a whim.

"Okay, you little rug rat. I've enjoyed spending the day with you but I've got to go now. You be good for your mom and no more wasting any of her delicious pie as face paint."

He covered the boy's rounded belly with one large, tanned hand.

Nathan kicked and laughed.

That made Adam do likewise. Laugh, not kick.

They had the same laugh, Josie noted. Soft and deep at first with a sort of raspy quality as it played itself out, growing quieter and quieter even though their faces remained bright and their bodies still shook. Finally it ended with a satisfied sigh.

"You don't have to run off on my account. If you want to spend more time with Nathan, that's all right with me. I have to get back to the café and set up for the dinner rush."

"Rush?" He cocked an eyebrow.

"Okay, trickle," she confessed. It was true that she did most of her business before one o'clock, but she did get a small flurry of activity around six when commuters stopped in to pick up take-home orders they had called in earlier in the day. Later another cluster of people would come in after their suppers to have pie for dessert. On really hot days she kept even busier because many thought it was worth the extra expense of eating out to avoid heating up their own homes.

Josie knew the people of this community. She knew their habits and their tastes, and it had paid off as much as it could. "But I can't afford to miss even a dribble of business these days."

"I realize that." He nodded. "Which is why I have to get moving."

"Moving?" The word made her shiver.

"Have a lot to get done, and now that my family knows I'm here, I don't have much time to do it."

"What's the supposed to mean?"

"It's not *supposed* to mean anything, Josie." His dark eyes fixed on her. His expression remained calm, but she could see the storm beneath the surface—as if what he felt and what he thought did not match up and he was going to have to reconcile them or choose. "I don't skirt around issues or try to pretty up the ugly truth. You know I came here for a reason, a reason I am not inclined to discuss with anyone." He handed Nathan back to her. "I will tell you this, though."

Josie pulled Nathan close. "What?"

"One of the reasons I don't want to tell you details about my plans is that, having met you now, having seen how you and Nathan fit into the fabric of Mt. Knott, I am not as sure of my intentions as I once was."

"That's a lot of words, Adam, but hardly any information."

He smiled, not too much and not with any joy in his eyes. "Maybe all you need to know, Josie, is that no matter what, from this point on I am not going to make a decision without taking you and Nathan into account first."

"Taking us into account is one thing. Taking us, um, that is, me into your confidence is quite another." She settled Nathan onto the floor in the front room to let him crawl around and play. As she bent forward the business card slid from her pocket and fell onto the ragged gold carpet. She snatched it up and went on with her point. "Taking us into account sounds nice, but really, it just means you are going to do what you decide anyway without asking me what I think."

He did not deny it or offer to do anything differently. He just brushed her cheek with his thumb and asked, "Did anyone ever tell you you're very wise for your age?"

She tapped the card against her open palm. "I've had to be to get by."

He nodded. "And now you have to do the wise thing and take the job cooking for this barbecue deal."

"You'd rather I not do this, wouldn't you?" She couldn't look down her nose at his not confiding in her if she didn't speak honestly with him.

"If it's just the money—"

"It's not." She held her hand up to cut him off, noticed the card in her fingers and folded her arms.

"If that's even a part of it, though, I could help you out on that score."

She took a step backward. "I can't take your money."

He looked down at Nathan, who had crawled to the couch and was trying to pull himself up into a standing position. "A case could be made that I owe you a year's worth of back child support."

"No. I don't see it that way." Josie shuffled one foot in Nathan's direction, ready to lunge out and nab him if he should fall. "You didn't know about him."

Adam shifted to the side, as well, only he seemed to be doing it in response to Josie, not a gut reaction to protect his child. "That doesn't change the fact that you had expenses."

"No. If we are going to start 'making cases'—" she paused and made quotation marks in the air "—in order to ease our guilt, then I should make one for the fact that I didn't track you down sooner to tell you about Nathan."

"I thought you didn't know about me until Ophelia sent you the adoption paperwork."

"I didn't. But I didn't make that effort either." She scanned the business card, the worn carpet, the baby who had just succeeded in pulling himself up onto his own two feet then promptly plopped back down onto his well-padded bottom. "And deep down I often thought that I should have made that effort. I may be naive about a lot of things. Innocent, even. But I do know it takes two people to make a baby, and I never once really tried to seek out Nathan's father."

"You are not just wise, Josie." He cocked his head. He studied her in much the same way he had on the first night they had met, but this time there was something more in his eyes. Respect. He didn't bother to conceal it when he said, with quiet conviction, "You are…amazing."

"Nope. Just someone trying to do the best I can, to be a good person and a good Christian."

"I know. You are."

"I try." She turned to watch Nathan again.

The baby grunted and groped at the couch cushion. He dug his tiny fingers into the fabric. His chubby legs bounced once, twice then his body jutted upward and he stood. "Ya-ya-ya!"

She smiled at her son. "Like everyone, I fail sometimes but I never stop trying."

"That's what makes you so wonderful."

Josie wished she could scoop her son up to take the attention away from herself. But she didn't want to take anything away from his hard-won accomplishment.

"You have to stop saying things like that or my head will swell up so big that I won't be able to get my café apron over it." She pantomimed putting on the apron that covered her from neck to knees.

"Ahh, you've caught on to my plan, to keep you from cooking for that barbecue."

They stood there in silence. Josie didn't know what to say or do.

Nathan lurched sideways for one step then another, his fingers curled into the soft cushion for support as he cruised toward the armrest.

Josie raised her head and now commanded Adam's gaze. She wanted to please this man but she was not ready to surrender that kind of trust to him. He had plans he would not tell her about and she had rent to pay.

"I won't take money from you." She laid it out as plainly as possible. "Not when I have a terrific way to earn it for myself. It's the right thing to do and won't cause you any hardship."

"I don't know about…" He stopped, looked down at Nathan, then back at her. "Wait. You think me paying your back child support would create a financial hardship for me?"

"Everyone in town knows you went through your inheritance right away."

"Oh, *everybody* knows that, do they?"

"You don't have to be ashamed. Like I said, we all fail. The important thing is to keep trying to do better."

He opened his mouth and raised his hand, like a man about to launch into a speech. Then his eyes shifted. His brow crinkled. He exhaled in a quick, hard huff. "I can't stand here and talk about this now, Josie. Just believe me when I say that if you should decide not to take the job, I will support you emotionally and financially in that choice."

Thump.

Nathan reached the end of the couch and sat down on the carpet, hard. He did not cry or fuss about it, just plunked down and sat there.

"It's not *just* about money, Adam." Now Josie did go to her child and pick him up. "It's also about me giving something back to the people who have been so kind to me."

His brow furrowed. "My family?"

"The people of Mt. Knott."

"Even if you have to take money from the people who have let the whole town down to do it?"

"I don't see them as having let the town down. They certainly did not want their business to flounder. I don't understand your animosity toward your father. As a father yourself now, it just seems that you'd be more forgiving."

He hung his head. "Maybe I haven't been a father long enough."

"But you've been a son for most of your life, a brother and a—"

"And a stray."

You don't have to be a stray, she wanted to say. *You have Nathan now. Nathan and me.* "Why can't you let go of that?"

He paused.

For a moment she thought he might break down, then he gathered himself, squared his shoulders and shook his head. "I have to go."

She could have offered to walk with him. He'd left his motorcycle behind the Home Cookin' Kitchen, after all, but she knew he wouldn't want to be seen with her and Nathan. A protective move, he'd say, but Josie could not make herself accept that without some reservation. So she watched Adam leave the house via the back door and disappear into the night without anything more demonstrative than a mumbled goodbye.

Ten minutes later she shut her front door behind her, not knowing what to do first about all this. Should she panic or praise the Lord?

Praise. Definitely praise.

Once she had spent a little time in prayer and thanksgiving, she would surely not feel so overwhelmed by everything and underequipped to deal with it. She had to stop and marvel at that notion. She had lived from one crisis to the next for so long, hung on by her virtual fingertips to survive from her childhood to her son's infancy.

But now she wasn't quite sure how to act when so much good news came her way. One thing after another, each brighter and more positive than the last. Who knew that even that would carry its own kind of stress? Have its own unique way of needing to lean on the Lord?

Josie hummed a hymn and walked toward the Home Cookin' Kitchen with a spring in her step that had not been there in a long, long time. She carried Nathan in her arms and from time to time he would lay his chubby cheek against hers as he gnawed his fist and "sang" along with her.

"Ya-ya-ya."

It wasn't exactly to the tune of "Blessed Be the Tie that Binds" but the child did manage to keep the right rhythm. Of course, every mother thought her own child was some kind of genius. And while Josie didn't see a musical career in Nathan's future, she did think he might have an affinity for listening and repeating.

"Ya-ya-ya."

"No. Not ya-ya. Try this, ma-ma."

"Ya-ya."

"No. No. Listen—" Josie pressed her lips together to sound it out. "Mmmma-mmma."

"Na-na-na."

"Mama." She hadn't encouraged the child to call her that before now. She couldn't. Not until…

Josie could not dismiss Ophelia's fickleness and that, until now, she had to be aware of the fact that there was an unknown father who could show up and take Nathan away. Now she had Adam's word, knew that his father was a sweet gentleman willing to welcome her into the family—if only on the fringes—and Ophelia's signature on the proper legal documents that meant that Nathan would soon be hers forever.

The only thing that could make this day better was to hear him form the name she hoped he'd call her for the rest of his life. "C'mon, Nath. Mama. Ma-ma-ma. Mama."

"Na-na-na."

"Mmmmmama. Ma-ma." She pointed to herself.

"Mmmmmya-ya." He pointed to himself.

"No, Nathan, that's me. Mama." Just saying it lifted her heart. So she pressed her fingertip more emphatically to her chest and said it again. "I'm your mama."

The child touched one finger to her face. "Ya-ya. Na-na. Da-da!"

"D-dada? Where did that come from?" Why was she asking him that? Even if he could have responded, Josie already knew the answer. "I have had you since the day you came home from the hospital. Walked the floors with you, prayed over you, spent every possible moment I could with you, and you call me the same thing you call your boo-boo bear and your big toe. He *has* you for a morning and a few hours in the afternoon and already you know the name, Da-da."

She hugged her boy close, not minding one bit that he had formed an instant and irrepressible bond with his father. Josie couldn't help noticing the man's charms herself.

"Dada. Da-da-da." He waved is hand around.

"Okay, I got it. Save it for when you see—" She followed the line of her son's finger and gasped. "Adam?"

Across the street from the Home Cookin' Kitchen and down about half a block was the unmistakable shape of a man in black standing by a gleaming Harley. He had his back to them and showed no probability of turning around, not when he was leaning with his forearm on a sleek silver car, talking to… someone. She couldn't see who.

"Not that it matters," she murmured to Nathan, thinking that even a one-year-old had to know she had really been talking to herself. "What the man does is his own business. Though…that doesn't *look* like business. Unless it's funny business."

Josie pulled Nathan close and stepped into the doorway of the vacant building next to the Home Cookin' Kitchen. She needed a moment to gather herself. She did not know what Adam was up to, though he'd made it clear he had no intention of telling her, so she couldn't be hurt by his need for privacy.

But the fact that it was *not* privacy that the man wanted but *secrecy,* that's what needled her.

She recognized the signs of it from all her years

dealing with her mother and Ophelia. Master manipulators, they always had schemes and small subterfuges working behind the scenes. Always had to be someplace, meet a person here or there, never in the open. Never on the up and up.

Josie's heart sank. She would not condemn Adam or write him off based on what little she did know. But she also could not simply believe in him blindly.

Adam had asked her to trust him and said he would take her into account when making decisions. But judging from his effort to get her not to cook for the barbecue and this sneaky behavior, the only thing he was taking into account was his own clandestine plans.

If it were just her, she might…but it wasn't just her. And if the adoption plans went well it would never be just her again.

Adam could promise to take her into account, but Josie didn't have a choice, she had to think of Nathan first and do what was best for him. That meant keeping both the doors of her business and the lines of communication between herself and the Burdetts open. And if Adam didn't like it, then…

A pang of guilt made her look in his direction just in time to see him point the way out of town, then step away from the silver car to reveal he had been speaking to a woman. A pretty woman. Poised. Even from this vantage point she gave off a sense of power and professionalism that Josie could never posses.

The woman started her car and pulled away from the curb.

"Dada."

"Shh. Nathan," she snapped.

The baby silenced.

"Mama's not mad at you, honey, it's just that…"

Adam got onto this Harley and took off, right behind the woman in the sleek sedan, without so much as a backward glance.

"I need to think." She tucked the child close and hurried to the front door of her well-lit diner, mumbling as she did, "Now, where did I put Burke Burdett's business card?"

Chapter Eight

"Thank you for meeting me out here on such short notice." Adam extended his hand to Dora Hoag. A compact, athletic woman with short black hair and the kind of personality that made people around her feel as if they were always running behind the power-walking, Bluetooth talking, multitasking, no-quarter-asking executive.

"It's just that once people know I'm in town it would only take a Web search to connect me to Global…"

"I understand your personal issues in all of this, Burdett." She didn't look at him when she spoke, so he was glad she'd used his name.

Dora tended not to look people in the eye unless they were her superiors or somebody she could get some good business out of. More than once Adam had almost commented on something she had said only to realize in the nick of time she was carrying on an electronic conversation and was hardly even aware of his presence.

She took only a moment to sweep her gaze over their surroundings.

Adam did the same.

He scowled that the half asphalt, half gravel parking lot that Adam had promised employees time and again they would finish off—only to have his father say it was fine the way it was—had not been fixed. And the long, low building painted buttery yellow and...well, the color had originally been called café au lait meant to evoke one of the flavors in their famed Crumble Pattie, had not been repainted in years. Now the butter color looked more like someone had mixed mud into vanilla ice cream, and the café au lait had sun-faded to a pinkish color not unlike the pancake makeup he'd seen elderly ladies wear to church. Separating the two colors was a border of bright blue-and-white checks and what was supposed to be an image of their lone product stamped like a large seal of approval to one side.

Corporate logos were supposed to be so easily identifiable that even without the red script "Carolina Crumble Pattie" emblazoned next to it, everyone who had ever seen the product would immediately recognize it. Adam had grown up making and eating that product and he still had no idea what the image on the building was supposed to be.

Luckily they had not used it in packaging or

anything official. One of the ongoing battles Adam had had with his father was about that very image. Adam had suggested they tap a fresh-faced local girl for the image of "Carolina Pattie"—and as he recalled that, Josie came to mind. But his father had flatly refused, not because Conner believed in the power of the disproportioned artwork but because he loved the artist, his wife, Maggie Burdett.

Adam had to force down the lump in his throat then. He looked away from the facade of the building and narrowed his eyes on the hills in the distance.

"But to me there is nothing personal at all here." Dora gave a sniff, frowned, then brought her full attention to bear on Adam, or as much of her attention as she gave to anyone in his position. "It's just business."

"But it won't be to my family." He motioned toward the back door marked Employees Only and pulled a key from his pocket. He unlocked the door, feeling a twinge of guilt about it. Dora didn't want to recognize the personal connection but she had no problem using it to give her a slight edge in her decision-making process. "My older brother and father would rather drive this business into the ground than to have to admit they needed me to broker the deal that would keep them afloat."

"That's why they are in the shape they are in." She crossed the threshold into the dimly lit hallway. "Can't run a successful business like that, right?"

Adam assumed she didn't actually expect him to

answer. Surely Dora had her own business opinions and theories.

He reached out and even in the darkness knew just where to find the light switch. It was a little like coming home to be here now. The comforting whirr of the fluorescent lights. The echo of their footsteps on the concrete floor. The familiar smell of the day's baking still lingered in the air.

Adam looked at the key in his hand, then down the length of the hallway with office doors on both sides. Then he searched beyond to the factory proper at the far end. Whether Dora wanted a response or not, he felt he had to say one thing. "They made a success of it for a lot of years."

"I know." There was an uncharacteristic kindness to her voice. Then she cleared her throat and took a step down the hall. "I've seen the profit-and-loss statements for the last decade. Mostly loss the last few years."

Adam squared his shoulders. "We can change all that."

"*Global* can change all that." She did not snap or come off defensive. If anything, Adam picked up a note of weariness, perhaps resignation in her reply. "And I know perfectly well what Global is capable of doing."

So did Adam, which was why he wanted to hear what Dora had in mind before Global went after the Crumble. They couldn't buy the company out if they didn't want to sell. Since the company was privately held, they could not force a hostile takeover.

What they could do was look at the company from every angle and see how they could make their own Crumble Pattie, bypassing the Burdetts altogether and undercutting their sales. That could put them out of business a full six months to a year sooner than the family would have managed to close the doors themselves. Or Global could come in, make a nice offer to take over the factory, let them keep their good name and take the Crumble Pattie to a national market as "one of the Global family of fine foods." They could save the company.

Except Adam suspected his father and brothers would not see it that way.

"On the up side of things, the Carolina Crumble Pattie factory turns out a very good product." She walked to the first office door and stopped to face it. Adam did not have to share her line of vision to know what name was painted in gold and black on the frosted glass: Conner Burdett—President. "They are a widely recognized brand in the region and a ready and loyal workforce."

"That hasn't changed," he reminded her.

"You don't have to sell me on this company, Burdett." A few more steps and a half turn put her in front of Burke's office door. She reached out to brush her fingertips over the name there. "I just needed to clap eyes on the physical locality before I make a rec-ommendation to the higher-ups."

"And that recommendation will be?" Burke's

deep voice startled Adam but seemed to have little effect on Dora.

Adam turned around and planted his feet shoulder width apart. He supposed the two of them looked a bit like old-time cowboys calling one another out in the street. Adam, who felt his features probably seemed darker and more menacing in the narrow hallway, stood six inches shorter than Burke, the tall fair-haired man with broad shoulders and unblinking blue eyes.

Adam did not react to his brother's looming presence with anything more than a quiet, "I suppose you want my key back?"

Burke let the door fall shut behind him. "I'd settle for an explanation for why you are here."

"I'd rather give you my key." Adam started to tug it off the key ring.

"Don't bother. If I had been worried about keeping you out I'd have changed the locks." That could mean more than one thing: the most likely being that Burke already knew about Adam's connection to Global and had prepared himself to handle it; or he was just toying with his younger brother, letting Adam know he would never be intimidated by a stray like him.

"I assumed you came here because *you* were worried," Adam challenged. "Somebody call and report seeing Dora's car and my Harley in the lot?"

Burke shook his head. "I came out to meet with

Josie Redmond about this fool barbecue deal Dad wants to throw."

Adam stepped back. "Josie?"

"She should be out here after she closes up."

"So, she is going through with that, then?"

"Was there ever any doubt?"

Yes. Adam had hoped she would turn his father down. Not just because he did not like the idea of her being in the middle of it all. Also since his brothers clearly had no inclination to organize the meal if Josie didn't pitch in, the whole event might just fall quietly by the wayside. "When is this barbecue?"

"Saturday," Burke said sounding more like a bull snorting than a man discussing a party.

"*This* Saturday?" Dora tipped her head and looked directly at the taller of the two brothers.

Burke nodded. Then he cocked his own head at the same angle as Dora's and said, "*You're* welcome to come."

Adam had not introduced Dora on purpose. He didn't plan on changing that now. "She won't—"

"I might just do that," Dora cut Adam off and held her hand out to Burke. "Dora Hoag."

"Burke Burdett."

Neither of them gave their business titles or bothered to share what relationship they had to the man they had in common, Adam. He couldn't help but feel a little left out over that.

She held Burke's hand longer than she'd ever held

a handshake, or even eye contact with Adam. "Does your company do this kind of thing for the community regularly?"

"Never," Adam muttered.

Burke did not let go of Dora's hand but waited for her to slip it away. Then he added, "And the old man isn't doing this for the *community*."

Dora looked from the older brother to the younger. "Oh?"

Burke squinted Adam's way. "It's a big party to honor the return of the favored son."

Adam pressed his lips together to spew out a curse. He caught a glimpse of his boss standing by watching with undisguised interest. Then he looked to Burke, who had spent a lifetime provoking all of the younger brothers and enjoying it far too much when Adam, inevitably, rose to the bait. He decided to forgo any gut reaction and respond with calm honesty. "*Me?* The *favored* son? Hardly."

"These days you are."

"No." He refused to believe that. "Being the singled-out son is not the same as being favored. I've never been favored in this town for anything, unless it was to let everyone down."

"That's not how I recall it. The old man and I have always butted heads. Lucky tries to stay below his radar. And the Hound…" Even though they had outgrown and/or rejected the designations long ago, Burke still called each of them by their old nicknames.

"Cody," Adam corrected quietly. "The old man has to be proud of Cody."

"Yeah. Sure. Pleased that the Hound found his calling and that he married a really nice girl. But less pleased that they are waiting to start a family until they have a church and anything but pleased that his preacher son is trying to influence him to apply Christian values to running the business."

"What's wrong with that?" Dora asked.

Adam and Burke both looked her way.

Her expression had changed, brightened while at the same time appeared more relaxed than Adam ever recalled her looking in the past. "Global sprang from a family business founded on Biblical principles."

Adam hadn't known that. It certainly didn't show in their current business model. Or did it? He had to admit to himself that he'd been so focused on his own goal he hadn't given that much thought.

"Interesting." Burke eyed her, sizing her up.

Burke sized everyone up. Adam had always had the impression that nobody ever measured up to his brother's standards.

"Maybe you can tell me how that has worked out for—" he gave her an almost admiring smile "—Global, did you say?"

Adam cleared his throat to take the heat off Dora. "Okay, so the old man is on the outs with Cody. That doesn't automatically move me up to the top of the heap."

Top of the dog pile was Burke's spot, and Adam concluded he wouldn't be able to resist making sure everyone, especially the woman who had caught the older brother's interest, knew it.

"No, that doesn't place you on top in Dad's eyes. But being the first of his boys to produce a grand-child *does*."

Once again his family proved him wrong.

Adam shut his eyes and rubbed the bridge of his nose. Every disclaimer he could dredge up, from Nathan not being a Burdett by blood to wondering how their father could accept a child born out of wedlock, faltered unsaid when Burke leveled his gaze on Adam and added, "You don't know what it means to him to hold at least one member of the next generation before he dies."

"He's too tough to die," Adam blurted out, all cavalier and full of bluster. But the bluster came not from the well of anger that had sustained him for far too long. Just acknowledging that his father had any weakness, much less that he would not be with them for years to come, left Adam feeling like a six-year-old kid, lost and afraid. "He's not…he's not sick is he?"

"Yeah. Heartsick," Burke said.

"Because of Mom?" Adam asked.

"Mom. You. The business. The town." Burke did not look Adam in the eye as he went down the list. "Your coming back and that baby are the first bright spots he's had in a very long while."

Adam swallowed hard and clenched his jaw to force back the emotion rising from his chest.

"Maybe I shouldn't be hearing this," Dora said softly, but she made no attempt to leave.

"Maybe you *should*." Burke did not say that he knew what she was up to, that he understood that she saw everything that mattered to him as a property, a product, an investment or a loss. "Maybe it wouldn't be such a bad thing if you knew a little about my father."

Adam stepped up. "Burke, that's not—"

Burke ignored him. "Everything that old man did, he did for this family. His family is still what matters most to him."

"Easy for you to say," Adam muttered, only, for once he felt no anger or animosity behind it.

"Maybe it is. Maybe it is easier for someone outside a situation to see it for what it really is. With that kid, you gave him the one thing no spreadsheet or year-end report or bank balance could ever provide—a glimpse into the future."

Adam did not know what to say to that. He knew Burke was right about his father and the family, yet he seriously doubted his own role in that family. How could he and a child he had produced, not from love and commitment and honor, but in a thoughtless run of sinful self-indulgence, mean anything to Adam's adoptive father? He meant the world to Adam already, of course, but to Conner Burdett? The child didn't even carry the name.

Yet.

Yet? Adam had never had a genuine "lightbulb" moment—where his dim view of the world suddenly became bright and clear as daylight in an instant—until now. Now standing in this building where he had literally grown up, where he had played with his brothers as a child and fought with them as a young adult, and torn away from them as a determined business man with his own ideas, Adam understood.

He owed it to Nathan to give him not just a name but a place in this family. Nathan deserved his part of the legacy that was the Burdett family and the Carolina Crumble Pattie Factory. The good, the bad…and the delicious.

He chuckled to himself at that.

"What?" Burke demanded, probably feeling defensive over the idea that Adam might be laughing at him.

Adam shook his head. "Nothing. You just opened my eyes a little bit, big brother." Adam slapped a hand on Burke's broad shoulder, and slapped it hard. He cared for the big lug but he hadn't turned to emotional mush. "I realize I have a lot more to accomplish while I'm in town than I had originally planned on."

"Then get out of here and get to it." He brushed Adam's hand off, but he did it with respect in his eyes.

That was new, Adam noted. He decided to test the depths of that respect. "I will. But I have to finish the job I came here to do."

Adam held his hand out to indicate Dora should accompany him down the hallway. "Ms. Hoag?"

"Hold it." Burke put his hand on Dora's arm. "You sold your shares in this place eighteen months ago. It's not yours to show to anyone."

"You plan to call security for your own brother?" Dora asked. She sounded more curious than concerned.

"No, ma'am."

Adam tucked his thumb into the waistband of his favorite pair of broken-in black jeans. He stood his ground.

"I don't need to call security to deal with my brother. I *am* the security that deals with him." Burke managed somehow to take up the whole breadth and height of the section of narrow hallway where he stood. "He'd do well to remember that."

"You haven't bested me since we got into it right after I graduated high school. And may I remind you, you always had a few years and five inches, and—" Adam stopped to look his brother over, taking a moment to show he'd noticed the way age had thickened the older man's midsection. He'd not gotten fat, by any means, but he wasn't the lean kid he'd once been. "And a few pounds on me."

"Not to mention a lot more smart." Burke tapped his finger to his temple and grinned.

"What's that supposed to mean?"

"It means I have enough sense to offer to spend

my evening with this lovely lady, showing her around the place and to tell you to get your tail out of here and go see how you can be of help to your son and Josie instead of hanging around where you don't belong like some—"

"Watch it," Adam warned.

"Stray dog," Burke concluded. "Be a man, Adam."

The knot in Adam's gut rivaled his fist for size and tension. If his boss hadn't been standing there calmly watching his every reaction, Adam might just have decked his brother then.

He eyed the bigger, beefier man head to toe and corrected himself. He'd have taken a swing at him. Made contact, even, then probably gotten the fire whipped out of him. Two years ago, even a week ago, Adam would have thought it would have been worth the pain and humiliation of defeat just to show his brother, or anyone, that he would back down to no one. Now?

Now Adam held his hand out to the man, not clenched in a fist but open and in a show of deference and gratitude. "I think I'll just do that. In fact, why don't we both be men and conduct ourselves and our business with one another the best way we know how. As Christians."

Burke eyed the hand. He scratched his chin. Clearly he knew that if he took Adam's hand now he was not just making an overture of reconciliation, he was pledging to act according to the principles they had both learned from their mother about morality, forgiveness and trust, among other things.

He hesitated, looked at Dora Hoag, who was studying him not unlike the way a scientist eyes a test subject, then he exhaled loud and gruff.

"Yeah." He grabbed Adam's hand and clamped down hard. "Okay."

"You all right with this, Ms. Hoag?" Adam asked.

"He's your brother. You tell me. Will I be all right?"

Adam chuckled. "If you can stand him, you'll be fine."

Dora Hoag *had* come to see the facilities. Adam knew she would reveal nothing about their business plans to Burke. Likewise, Burke would not tell Dora any secrets that might throw the deal in either direction. It would, in fact, be either a quiet tour or one that veered off into more personal territory. Who knew where that might lead? Maybe a year from now Adam would be in Mt. Knott running the plant and Burke would be traveling the country in charge of acquisitions.

Besides, Burke would be within his rights to throw them both off the premises. Leaving her here with his brother actually seemed the best solution.

"If you hurry you can get to Josie before she closes up." Burke reached into his jeans pocket and pulled a folded piece of yellow legal paper out. "Give this to Josie. It's more budget, cost-per-guest type of thing, than a menu. All I care about is, is there is enough food out here by noon Saturday to feed every hungry mouth that shows up. I'll leave the actual food part up to her."

Dora looked at him as if that had told her something significant about the man.

"What can I say?" Burke shifted his shoulders and settled his thumbs in his belt loops in an "aw shucks" manner that belied the hardened business acumen lurking beneath the surface. "I'm a number cruncher not a chef."

"Don't buy that act," Adam told Dora with a smile.

She shook her head. "Don't you worry about me."

Adam laughed, quietly. "Yeah, he may be Top Dawg around here but I've seen you in action, Ms. Hoag. You are the Alpha Shark in a sea full of circling man-eaters."

For half an instant it dawned on Adam that Ms. Hoag, not the savvy businesswoman, but the just plain old smitten woman, might not have wanted that kind of image put before Burke.

But she laughed, gave Burke a look that promised Adam meant every word then turned to the younger brother and looked him in the eye for the first time maybe ever. She said, "I will see you at the barbecue, Burdett. And I can make you this promise. I'll give you my recommendation there, before I turn it official."

It was a courtesy Adam had not earned by rank or familiarity, so he appreciated it all the more. Despite her claims of it not being personal, she was granting him the chance to know what she would say, what Global would most likely do, before anyone else knew.

Once that would have made him so proud, given him a sense of power over his family. Now it felt like a heavy burden to bear. Not because anything had changed about his father or his family or how they felt toward him. He was still the outsider. The one who no longer had a stake in their livelihood and who had never had a place in their hearts, the stray.

But Adam had changed, just a little.

He *wasn't* a stray.

He was a father now, and he had to start acting like it, starting with going to Josie and supporting her in doing what she thought was right for herself, the people she cared about and her son. Even if what she thought was right meant catering to and collaborating with his family.

Chapter Nine

Josie stood back from the blackboard wall. She pulled the scrunchie from her ponytail and sighed in relief as the curls fell around her shoulders and the tightness eased from her scalp. She replayed her earlier phone conversation with Burke Burdett.

She had to whip up every last ounce of courage to make the call, partly because she knew Adam hadn't wanted her to do it. But mostly because, of all the Burdett brothers, whose reputations were considerable in this town, Burke was the most…the biggest… the…well, he didn't just *like* the nickname Top Dawg, the man *lived* it. He had to take the lead in every situation, every conversation and he had to come out on top of every transaction, deal or exchange. What chance did a girl like Josie stand with a man like that?

Pretty good, it turned out, once he'd learned that

Adam had offered her money to not take the job. She hadn't meant to tell him that. It had just slipped out. But after it had, the man had gone to great lengths to accommodate her.

She would have liked to tell him she had never known that kind of rivalry for a sibling who, while you worked and followed the narrow path, chased after their own interests and still ended up your parent's darling while you went unnoticed. But she understood the feeling exactly and he knew it.

That fact had gone far to forming an unspoken bond between them. Burke wanted to get every last detail of this party right, and when she thought of Adam with that polished and poised businesswoman, she wanted that, too. It might be a party to commemorate Adam's return, but it was going to give Josie and Burke each a chance to shine. Whatever good it would do them.

So Burke had been particularly open to her suggestions when she explained her plan to use her suppliers for the food and sundries and enlist the help of the locals to get the "fixin's" to the tables.

Burke had told her he didn't care how she did it. As their official caterer she just needed to get it done right. Still, she felt bad about not cooking everything herself. However, given the short notice and the number of pies they would need to feed the crowd, it was the only realistic solution. Besides, Josie loved the idea of the community showing the Burdetts just what they could do when they all pulled together.

"This just might work." She studied the complex maze of columns, lines and arrows charting out how to supply enough food for the celebration.

"Oh, good. You're not closed yet." Adam came striding in with such confidence that she knew he couldn't have imagined for one second that he'd find that door locked.

"Just sorting out some details before…" Somehow admitting where she was headed after closing felt like a bit of a betrayal. Only, Josie couldn't say exactly who it was she thought she'd be letting down—Adam or Burke. Or herself. "Give me your honest opinion."

"Always."

"Do you think potato salad is a salad or a side?"

"What?"

Josie rolled her eyes at her own feeble attempt at diversion. She'd never been any good at anything that required her to be socially adept or coy. That was Ophelia's area of expertise. Josie had admired that about her sister, except for how her sister sometimes used it to take advantage of others.

She looked at the square-shouldered man who had obviously found much to appreciate about Ophelia, as well.

Still, she'd started this, so she had to stumble through it.

"Um, you know, potato salad?" She pantomimed eating as if she thought the man spoke another language, or perhaps had once been seen using globs of potatoes and mayonnaise as a hat and needed to know she meant the *other* kind of potato salad. "Would you classify it as a salad or a side dish?"

"Why would I want to do either?"

"Well, *you* wouldn't but *I* have to." She stepped back and showed him the convoluted columns on the wall. "See, I've just about worked this all out." She waved her hand like a game-show model. "But there is sort of a...hiccup in the division of salads-versus-side-dishes. We're heavily weighted toward side dishes."

He squinted at the board and made a noncommittal, "Hmmm."

"It's probably fine. I think we'll have enough food if everyone brings what they are assigned."

"Looks like you've got it all figured out." He turned toward the wall.

She stared at the squiggles and notations, waiting for him to say something about it all. To point out that if she had been ethical enough not to take money from him for something she didn't deserve, she shouldn't take it from his family for the same reason. She wasn't doing the majority of the cooking, after all.

Maybe he'd find some other fault with her decision.

Or maybe he didn't care at all, especially since he had a real lady friend in town.

The longer they went without speaking, the more the situation, or the nonsituation, built up in her mind. If she let it go on much longer who knew what wild story she would concoct? A potato-salad conspiracy?

Bank loans being called in before the barbecue check arrived? Adam choosing the woman in a silver sedan to step in as Nathan's stepmother?

"I had to do it, Adam." The words rushed out. "It was just good business. The way things are in Mt. Knott, turning down this amount of business just wouldn't be smart."

He looked at her at last, a twinkle in his eyes. "Well, no one ever accused me of being smart,"

"Don't feel bad. Some folks have to be content to be just another pretty face," she teased him right back. As soon as the words left her mouth she felt the heat rise in her face like some silly schoolgirl. Socially adept as Ophelia, she was not. "Uh, you'd better go. I have to lock up and see if I can get someone to watch Nathan before I go out to discuss all this with your brother."

"All this?" He held his hand out. "Salads and hiccups and all?"

"Uh-huh."

"As has been pointed out not that long ago, I am not the smart one 'round these parts, but wouldn't it have been smoother to have him come here and see this for himself?"

She gave a shrug. "He's the boss."

Adam's mouth tightened. "Fair enough," he relented. "But right now your boss is busy with my boss."

"Your…does she happen to be a very well-put-together lady?"

"Well, I've never checked her for patches or busted seams—"

"I'm glad to hear that!" Josie slapped her hand over her mouth before her ineptitude got her into further trouble.

Adam grinned. "But, yes, Ms. Hoag comes off as very well pulled together."

"Comes off as? Meaning looks can be deceiving?"

"Lots of things can be deceiving," he said enigmatically. "But this 'look' is on the up and up."

Josie nodded. "So, what does that mean for me?"

She forced herself not to put her hand over her mouth again. She was asking what Adam's boss being with *her* boss meant for her, not what Ms. Hoag's "look" and association with Adam meant to her. If he didn't gather that then…then maybe she'd have some of her most burning questions answered.

"It means I get to bring you this." He held out a piece of folded paper. "It's the budget for the party that Burke worked up on your preliminary information."

"Oh?" She took the paper and unfolded it slowly.

"If it's not right, if you need more money or autonomy, leave it to me. I'll fix it. I'll make sure my family does right by you, Josie."

But who will make sure you *do right by me?* Never a slow learner, Josie had managed to keep that remark entirely to herself. Still, she did wonder…

"What do you think?"

"Think?" She had kept the remark silent, right?

"About Burke's figures."

"Oh." She took a minute to read over the paper. Burke had been quite generous with her, but not so much that she would have felt compelled to argue the money. "I think I can work with this."

"Really? And get it all done by Saturday at noon?"

"I'm closing down after the coffee rush tomorrow, and I'm going to make pies into the wee hours of the night."

"You poor kid."

"No! I can't wait. I'm looking forward to it. The chance to do what I love and the one thing I know I am good at."

"One thing? No way." He moved closer to her. So close he could brush the freshly undone curls off one shoulder as he said with quiet intensity, "Josie you're great at so many things…"

"How would you know?"

"I just do. You're a good mom, I know that and…"

"And that's enough for now." She held up her hand and retreated from him. "It really means a lot to hear you say that, though."

He only nodded, his hand still in the air at shoulder level for a moment before he let it fall to his side.

"That's one reason I'm so excited about tomorrow." She took a chatty tone, hoping to take control of things again. She walked briskly toward the front door, hoping Adam would follow and be on his way. "I get to do the work I love, knowing it will be enjoyed by the people I love, plus I get to have Nathan nearby all day."

He did follow, a bit too closely.

When she turned around, she found herself just inches away from the man. "What…could be… better?"

"What indeed?"

"What indeed?" she murmured. Then, coming to her senses before she gave in to the deep, soothing masculinity of his voice, she gave the door a push and cool air rushed in around them. "I know. It sounds completely corny to a man like you."

"A man like me?"

"A man of the world."

"Harsh words."

"Harsh? That you're educated, well-spoken, well traveled, experienced and sophisticated?"

"That I am 'of the world' when *you* so clearly need a man willing to come out of the world and separate himself from its ways."

She smiled slightly to hear him paraphrase the Biblical admonition that Christians should be apart from the world. "I was thinking more that you're worldly and I'm…Mt. Knotty."

"You're the last person I'd consider naughty," he teased. "In fact, I'd vote you Most Likely to be Nice."

"Knottish, then." She gave him a good-humored scowl.

"Knottish or not at all, I'm in the very same boat

as you there." He put his hand on the door and raised his face to the summer breeze. "I grew up right here in Carolina countryside. Except for this last year and a half in Atlanta I haven't lived anywhere else. I spent my holidays here, my summer vacations and made this my home after college."

"I guess I never thought of that." Josie stared out into the fading light of evening. "I always pictured the Burdetts as having a different kind of lifestyle than the rest of us."

"We did. Still do, I suspect." His arm still braced to prop the door open, he narrowed his eyes at the blackboard wall. "Where the rest of you got to clock out and leave the factory behind you, we all carried the responsibilities with us all the time. As a kid I used to ride my bike straight to the Crumble, did my homework in my dad's office, then went home with my mom for dinner then back to help my dad lock up."

"Oh, Adam, that is so sad."

"Sad? How so?"

"Sort of missed out on your childhood, didn't you?"

"And your childhood, Josie?"

She shook her head. "I sort of missed out on my childhood, too. Though I don't know that Ophelia would say she missed out on hers."

"Personally, I think she may still be living hers."

"Adam!" Josie had thought the exact same thing, but it was the age-old conundrum about brothers and sisters. You can say whatever you feel about them, but just let someone else try it and suddenly you'll defend your loved one. "Ophelia must have matured some. Otherwise why would she have signed the papers allowing me to adopt Nathan and finally shared the information about his father?"

"About *me*," he corrected.

She pressed her lips together.

He bowed his head for a moment, then looked again out into the serene small-town setting.

Josie put her back against the other side of the door frame and crossed her ankles. "At least when you were doing all those things, you were doing them here, in a safe home, a nice town and with your family. I was dropped off in Mt. Knott and only saw my mother now and then, and Ophelia almost never."

"I guess I do have *that* to be thankful for."

Ophelia wasn't the only one showing more maturity, Josie thought. Two days ago Adam would have used that opportunity to lambaste his family or make a joke about their rocky relationships.

"It's not that bad, now that I have—" her gaze met his "—now that I have Nathan. And I hope that Ophelia will come around in time. I wrote her a nice long thank-you letter when she signed those papers and told her she was welcome to visit us anytime."

"And you think she will take you up on that?" His eyes grew dark. His back went straight.

Josie wasn't sure if it was hope or horror in his voice.

"She's my sister, Adam. I can't forget that."

"Neither can I," he said softly. "You may think of me as a man of the world, but I'm just as humbled and confused by all of this as you are, Josie."

"So if we're not worldly what does that make us?" she asked.

"A couple of Mt. Knott-heads?" Laughter mingled with the more somber emotions in his expression.

"A couple of workaholics." She checked her watch. They'd both put in more than a full day's duty and it wasn't even dark yet. Realizing he wasn't going to take the hint and walk out, Josie headed inside. Full day's work or not, she still had to close down.

"So what do we do about that?" he asked.

"Do?" She flipped the lock shut and turned the Open sign to the Sorry, We're Closed side. "About what?"

"About all work and no play making us dull folks."

She headed for the cash register, wondering if she could just pull the drawer, lock it in the vault and count the money in the morning. "I don't think anyone has ever described you as dull, Adam Burdett."

"Would it shock you to say that sometimes I wish they would?"

Ching.

She stood with her hand hovering above the register key that had just opened the drawer. "Yes. I can think of a lot of other words I'd use for you, but *dull?* I just can't see it."

"What words?"

"Hmm?" She wrestled the money compartment free and clunked it on the counter.

He stood at her side now. "What words would you use for me?"

She gave the stacks of bills, all ones and fives, a quick reckoning. "*Strong. Decent.* Maybe a little bit—" she lifted the top half of the compartment to check underneath for checks and twenties and found one of each "*—dangerous.*"

He did not contest that.

She started to turn to take the drawer to the back, then her curiosity got the better of her. She had to know. "What words would you use to describe me?"

"You? Hmmm. That's tough."

"Oh, yeah?"

"Ex-peshully for a pretty-faced country dawg like me, ma'am, who ain't got a very big vol-cab-ulurry."

"Maybe if I held up a treat and commanded you to speak?" She sank her teeth into her lower lip.

"Do I get to choose what you use for a treat?"

"Okay. I get it. I'm too…*me* for words." She spun around and headed into the kitchen, intent on putting the money in the back room, gathering up her sleeping child, getting home and putting this day—and this man—behind her.

"*Capable.*"

"What?" She looked up as her shoulder touched the office door and found him right beside her.

"One of the words I'd use is *capable*."

"Well, isn't that…utilitarian?" She stepped into the small room and set the money on the desk.

"And *smart*," he added, following her inside.

"Better," she plucked the key to the vault off the hook, then turned and found she couldn't take another step.

"And—" he leaned in *"—kissable."*

Moments before he could put his lips to hers she had to whisper. "But I'm not Ophelia."

"What?"

"I may be the things you described me as, but the one thing I am not…is Ophelia."

"I know that."

"Then you will understand why I can't let you kiss me now."

"I will?"

"If you'll excuse me I have got to finish up in here and take Nathan home."

"Now?"

"Yes, now. He's already asleep, and I'd like to get him to his crib."

"No. You said you can't let me kiss you *now*. Does that mean you can let me kiss you eventually?"

Josie hesitated.

"Ah, c'mon, give a guy some hope."

"Adam," she whispered. "It's too fast. It's too… much. We have to think about Nathan and his custody." *Then there is the whole Ophelia issue.* "We can't just give in to our feelings for each other without taking things like that into account. It's too soon."

She marched to the door. "If you don't mind. I have to lock up before I leave."

"Let me see you home."

"I can manage the short walk." She shoved him out the office door. "But if you want to spend some time with your son, come by here tomorrow afternoon. There might even be something sweet in it for you."

"Ahh, hope springs eternal." He put his hand to his heart.

"I'm talking baked goods," she called after him.

But he didn't seem to hear a word of it.

Chapter Ten

Adam belted out his own version of "That's Amore" with a tribute to "Josie's apple pie" as he swung open the front door of the Home Cookin' Kitchen.

Everyone in the whole room, including Nathan in his portable playpen in the corner, fixed their eyes on him. Mouths gaped open.

He paused in the open doorway. "What? Can't a man face the day with a song in his heart?"

"If it stays in his heart," Jed grumbled.

"Once it starts spilling out past his teeth and starts getting stuck into the ears of innocent bystanders, them innocent bystanders got a right to make a comment."

"And your comment is?" Adam asked.

The two older fellows exchanged glances before they spoke as one, saying, "Shut your pie hole!"

"Aw, leave him alone. I like this side of him. Better than that strong, silent type skulking about on that noisy motorcycle," said a woman standing at the table of coffeepots, pouring cream into a steaming thermal cup.

"I like the *other* side of him," Warren gruffly proclaimed.

"The other…" Adam looked over his shoulder at his supposed "other" side.

Now all eyes moved to Warren.

"What are you talking about?" Jed shifted his weight to one stool away from his regular spot at the counter.

Warren coughed. "I'm talking about the side of him we all see when he's heading out the door."

Jed grunted to show his disbelief.

"Seems that's what them Burdetts do the best, anyway. When things get tough they turn tail and save themselves."

"That's not fair, Warren." Josie came through the kitchen door wiping her hands on her apron.

"Ain't fair that after twenty years at the Crumble my wife now has to work all hours catering to teen-agers in a bowling alley in another town, either."

"Have you ever stopped to think how much time each of the Burdetts has spent trying to keep the business afloat?" she asked. Her gaze flicked up to meet Adam's, then just as quickly she looked away.

"Afloat? That explains a lot." Jed snorted and retook his regular seat. "We thought they was making snack food, *they* thought they was building bass boats!"

"Hey, hey! Paychecks from that factory paid for most of the bass boats sitting in driveways around this town. They didn't plan for things to go sour out there." Josie threw the towel down.

"Maybe they should have." Warren swiveled around to look at Adam head-on at last. "Sour snacks were a big trend for a time. Maybe if the Burdetts had just once considered adding to the line of products…"

"Well, I have heard of backseat drivers and armchair quarterbacks, Warren, but never diner-stool businessmen. You haven't even taken into account—"

"No, Josie, don't feel you have to defend us." Adam held his hand up. "I agree with the man. The Burdetts could have done better by this community."

Adam could have gone on about how he felt the Burdetts had treated him personally or taken this opportunity to tell the townspeople about his hopes for turning things around. But since he could not, in his own heart, untangle the two, he did not trust his motives for saying anything.

Funny, a few days ago, before meeting Josie and seeing the way she tried so earnestly to live her faith, Adam would never have questioned that. He'd have spoken his mind, no matter who it hurt or why he said it. "I guess if that means y'all would rather not have me around while you have your breakfast, I'd understand."

"Naw. I've had to stomach Jed's ugly mug all these

years." Warren jerked his thumb toward his old friend. "I can stand a Burdett for a few minutes, I reckon."

"That's his indirect way of saying he appreciates your honesty," Jed translated.

"Thank you very much." Adam gave a nod, then launched into his song again.

"I appreciate your honesty, pal, but not your singing," Warren tacked on good and loud.

Everyone laughed.

Josie put her hands over her ears. "Would you stop making all that racket?"

She caught his eye and smiled.

He did not know if the redness of her cheeks came from their gazes meeting or from the heat of her defending his family name or from her work in the kitchen where she had just been baking. She cocked her head, and her topknot of curls wobbled. She batted away a loose strand of hair and left a smudge of flour on her nose.

Adam had never seen a more beautiful woman in his life.

She stooped to pick up Nathan and settled the fat baby on her hip.

No, Adam amended his original conclusion, *now* she was the most beautiful woman he'd ever seen.

"Assistant pie chef reporting for duty." Adam gave her a snappy salute.

"You?" Jed scoffed.

"Yeah. Me." He lowered his hand slowly.

"But this is baking." Josie waved her hand, scattering a fine puff of flour through the air. "It's not something I associate with a Harley-riding bad-boy type."

"Bad boy?" On one hand he wanted to point out neither adjective fit him. On the other, he found it kind of cool that she saw him that way. Women loved bad boys, right? "Does that mean you want to tame me?"

"Hmmm." She put her hand on her hip and cocked her head. Her curls bounced against her head. "Maybe if you traded that motorcycle in for a minivan."

"Hold the phone, Sweetie Pie. What goes on here?" Jed swiveled around on his stool. "Most women wait until they've got a fellow's ring on their finger before they go trying to change him."

Minivan?

Ring?

Whoa!

He'd come back to Mt. Knott to claim his kid and show his detractors exactly what he was capable of—succeeding where they had failed. Not to go the home-and-hearth route with…

Adam looked to the woman setting his son down. Yeah, he had wanted to show everyone just what he was capable of. Why did he suddenly think he might be capable of so much more than he himself had ever suspected?

"I grew up in a food-prep industry." He approached the counter, spotted Nathan standing in his playpen, bent down and said to his son, "Explain to your mom, please, that I can manage to turn out a few edible pies."

"Edible? I hope my pies are a little better than just edible."

"You notice they never touched the marriage and man-changing issue?" Warren stroked his chin.

"Completely tap-danced all the way around it." Jed waggled two downward-pointing fingers to demonstrate the deftness of the pair's maneuvering.

Adam held both hands up. "Hey, I came here and volunteered to handle freshly baked pies, not hot potatoes."

Warren laughed. "You're all right, Burdett."

Jed joined him. "He has our stamp of approval, Sweetie Pie."

"Great. Then why don't y'all stick that stamp on real tight, take him down to the post office and see if you can send it off to parts unknown for a while. Because nobody gets in my kitchen while I make pies."

"She's afraid you'll learn her secret ingredient," came the jovial voice of an older woman at Adam's back. The aroma of coffee curled up in the steam from her mug.

"If I was her I'd be afraid he'd steal more than that," a younger woman pouring sweetener from a pink packet chimed in.

Josie's face went a deeper shade of red.

Adam chuckled.

Neither of them denied her statement.

"I think we'd better add Josie's name to the prayer list, then." The older woman clamped the lid down on her thermal cup and headed toward the wall.

Adam turned to look at the column on the blackboard wall. He opened his mouth to make a joke. Then closed it, humbled, and simply read the requests in silence.

"Please, please, pray that my mom keeps her job. Kyle"

"Remember those who have lost health insurance, that we all stay well. Elvie"

"Please pray I find work." That followed by not one but an entire list of names.

After so many selfish and anger-blinded years, the problems of the Burdetts and Mt. Knott suddenly felt bigger than Adam's pain. That was Josie's doing, he decided. No, that was so much bigger than Josie.

He scanned the list again, and found something that made his breath still.

"Please pray for Adam Burdett." No signature.

Yes, he had felt lonely and rejected, ignored and unloved. Well, welcome to the world. So many hearts bore those burdens and yet they stopped and took the time to pray for others, to come together, to help each other.

"You don't have to add our Sweetie Pie to any list," Jed said softly. "She's always in our prayers."

The rough older men narrowed their eyes at Adam.

He twisted around to meet their silent admonition with a somber look. He got it. And he wanted them to know it.

Jed nodded in acknowledgment first.

Warren took longer but when he raised his cup to recognize the promise that had passed between them, it warmed Adam to his gut.

Then Josie clapped her hands together. "All right. That's enough of that. Everyone fill your cups, add your sugar and cream and settle up your bills, please. I'm ready to lock up for the rest of the day."

"Which side of the door do you want me on when the lock slides into place?" Adam asked quietly.

Josie frowned, well, as much as she ever frowned. It was more a cross between a pout and a playfully sour face.

Adam grinned at her.

She sighed and shut her eyes.

He didn't know if she was saying a prayer, gathering her strength to do what she had to do or blocking him from view so she could think straight. Maybe all three. But when she finally opened her eyes again, she was smiling.

"I want you on this side." She pointed to the spot beside her.

"Fantastic! Get me an apron and call me the Mt. Knott doughboy!"

"Oh, you can have an apron but you aren't getting anywhere near my dough."

Josie hit a button on the cash register, and the drawer popped open with a *ding!*

"So what job do you have in mind for me? Cherry picker? Apple slicer? Peach peeler?'

"I was thinking more gopher."

"I know this is the South but I don't think even here that anyone will want gopher pie."

"The gopher won't be in the pie—the gopher will be in your apron."

"Won't that make it more difficult for me to get any work done?"

"Going for things that I need will be your job. That and watching Nathan."

"Never thought I'd see the day," Jed laid down his payment plus a little extra. He made a sign to Josie to indicate she should keep the change. "Nope. Never thought I'd see the day when a Burdett would do the bidding and get ordered around by one of their own laid-off workers."

"Sorta gets a guy right here." Warren pounded his chest as he headed out onto the street.

"So does indigestion," Adam called as he held the door open for the departing customers.

"Yeah. But there's a tonic for indigestion," Warren said. "For what you've got, son…?"

He and Jed both shook their heads.

"…ain't no remedy on Earth for that," Jed concluded. "Nothing to take for it."

"Oh, I don't know. He could try taking some vows." Warren laughed.

Adam gulped. *Vows?* He cared about Josie, even having only recently gotten to know her. But vows? "Look, I admire Josie's pluck and appreciate the job she's done with Nathan, but…"

"Don't underestimate what it means to find a woman who is a good mother to your child."

"And your child ain't actually *her* child."

"It don't hurt when she's prettier than a speckled pup."

"And cooks better than your own mama."

"Josie's a good woman."

"And we expect you to be good to her."

"I will. But I'm not ready for marriage."

"Apparently you wasn't ready to be a daddy, neither, but here you are."

"Here I am."

"Maybe you ought to take a good long look at yourself before you settle your mind on what you are and are not ready for."

Adam turned and looked at himself reflected in the glass door.

Apron.

Baby.

Giving up an entire day to spend time with a woman giving him orders and turning up the heat and turning away his advances.

And he didn't mind any of it.

Well, he would have liked it better if she'd let him kiss her. But he understood and respected her choices.

That fact alone gave him pause. Maybe those older fellows had a point. Maybe he did need to take a good long look at himself before he made up his mind about himself and Josie.

Chapter Eleven

"Do me a favor?" Josie stepped to the doorway, the first of many freshly baked pies in her silicon-mitted hand.

Adam looked up from a rousing round of a game that might be called "see Daddy scramble after every toy Nathan throws on the floor" and made the bug-eyed bear in his hand squeal with one well-timed squeeze. "Anything."

"First, stop chasing down everything he throws."

"Just trying to make myself useful."

"As what? A Labrador retriever?"

Adam looked at the bear then back at Josie. "Woof."

She laughed. "You're supposed to be the one in charge. Do you really think that if you go after everything the instant he tosses it overboard you are teaching him the way things work in the real world?"

"The *real* world?" Adam scowled. "He's a baby. Why does he need to know about the real world?"

"Because that's the world we are all born into. We have so little time to get his feet on the right path, with so many things trying to get him to stray…"

"What if straying comes naturally to him?" Adam flipped the bear over and over in his hands.

Adam was testing her and she knew it. Just as Nathan might push something away or even throw it aside.

"Straying comes naturally to all of us." She glanced around her at the tables and chairs that would, on a normal Friday, be just now filling up with the lunch crowd.

She had served her friends, her fellow townspeople and strangers day in and day out. She had sat next to many of these same people in town meetings and church services. But here, where they had not always been on their best behavior, they had taught her something more precious than any of them knew.

Her eyes went to the prayer list and she managed a slight smile. "Isn't that why Jesus is known as the Good Shepherd? We need Him to watch over us and bring us back into the fold when we lose our way."

"Why, Miss Josie, I didn't expect a Sunday school lesson from you today." His mouth quirked up on one side, half in humor, half in challenge to her. Another test.

Would she pass it? Would she stand up to him? And, more important, stand up for her beliefs?

"Didn't expect a lesson, but I notice you didn't say you didn't *appreciate* getting one."

"You are a wonder, Josie." He laughed.

"Takes one to know one," she joked.

"Me? A wonder?" He dropped the toy into the playpen with the baby, then took a few steps toward the counter. "Only if by that you mean I *wonder* if I'll ever get the hang of this Daddy stuff."

"I think you will."

"Do ya?" he asked softly, his eyes dark and his smile a very masculine mix of smug and wistful.

"Yeah, maybe by the time he goes off to college," she teased.

Adam opened his mouth, probably to protest or to at least boldly proclaim his belief in his own parenting abilities when Nathan let out a *"Ph-th-th-th-ppp-ttt"* and sent the bear sailing right at the side of Adam's head.

The bear hit its mark then slid to the floor.

He gazed down at the thing then at the baby, who stood with his pudgy fingers flexed and wriggling in the direction of the bear.

"Sorry, kiddo. Game over."

Nathan grunted in anger and stretched up on his toes, his arms rigid and his cheeks red.

Adam plopped the bear on the counter. "Next time maybe you'll realize that if you really want something you have to hang on to it. Don't let it go. And certainly don't throw it away and assume you can have it back whenever you want."

Nathan shrieked.

Adam did not budge. "Listen to your ol' dad. This is a subject he knows something about."

Josie froze. What exactly had Adam thrown away, then wished he could get back again? Not Nathan, as he had never known about the child. Ophelia? She held her breath to think of it.

"Okay, got that." Adam now turned his full attention on her. "What else can I do for you? You just name it."

Fall in love with me and become Nathan's father in every sense of the word forever and ever. She leaned against the door frame and sighed over her indulgent little fantasy. Her and Adam and Nathan. Their own patchwork of a family. Visiting with the other brothers and their families, if any of them ever had any, on holidays. Watching Nathan grow and perhaps giving him a sister or brother or both. Sharing a home and a future. Going to church together. Going to…

The smell of pies ready to be taken from the oven brought her back to reality. "Um, if you don't mind, would you taste this pie?"

"I don't mind. But I have tasted your pie before. It's delicious."

"When I bake a few at a time, it's delicious. But trying to make enough for this barbecue? I've never tried to mix up that much pie crust before. I'm not sure I got the right ratio of flour to—"

"Yes?" He arched an eyebrow.

"Oh, no. You are not getting my secret recipe out of me that easily." She slid the pie pan onto the counter, then turned around to retrieve a knife and a pie server. "Not unless you can figure it out for yourself."

"If I do—" he sat himself at the counter and picked up a fork "—will you finally tell me your secret, Josie?"

"I'll tell you mine if you'll tell me yours." It came out before she could stop herself. And then she was glad she had *not* stopped herself. Because of all the things she wanted from Adam, knowing his secrets, knowing the undeniable truths upon which he based his decisions was right up there.

"Let me have a taste of that pie." He did not promise to share anything with her.

She slid the stainless steel server in under the crust of the small triangular piece she had cut from the whole. Slowly she lifted it up, then lowered it slowly, then lifted it again. It had the right heft.

She closed one eye and peered at it with the other eye narrowed as if scanning the thing with a laser beam. It had the right look.

She closed both eyes now, pulled back her shoulders and inhaled. It had the right aroma.

The top and bottom crust broke into delicate flakes just as they should. The filling clung to the chunky upper crust that was her trademark, in the way it always did, with the fruit still firm and plump, not watery or crushed under the weight of the top. Still, Josie would not be satisfied that she had done her best until she heard it from someone whose opinion mattered to her.

That thought made her take a sharp right turn with the pie plate still in hand. "Here, Nathan, you take the first bite."

"Hey! What about me?"

"This is your chance to show your son how to practice patience by example," she returned, aiming to appear witty when, in fact, she was terrified.

She was a mother. A mother who had lived the past year in fear that at any moment her child could be taken from her. Now, just when it seemed she could put that fear behind her and move on to build a life for herself and her child, this man comes along. Yes, Nathan's father, but also a virtual stranger to Josie. A stranger, by his own admission, with a secret.

She could not afford to take that lightly. Nor could she allow her own feelings alone to dictate her actions. She had to get her priorities right and keep them right. No matter how she felt about this man, she was first and foremost Nathan's mother.

She pinched off a bite just right for a one-year-old and poked it into Nathan's mouth.

He worked it around with his tongue more than with his tiny front teeth. Some of the red dribbled onto his chin, and he rubbed his fist over it and began to gnaw at his balled-up fingers. "Mmmm-nnnnmmmm-nop-nah-nnop."

"Does that mean he likes it or not?" Adam moved in close behind her and then leaned forward to peer at the child, bringing him closer still.

"I don't know," she confessed, her eyes glued on the boy's reaction in a gargantuan effort not to sense how close Adam was standing. Not to smell the still-fresh line-dried scent of his apron or hear the jingle of his change and keys when he put his hand in his pocket.

"Ya-ya-ya!" Another shriek, then Nathan went on tiptoe and stretched his arms out for the plate in Josie's hand.

"I think he likes it." Adam laughed

Josie laughed, too, and offered her son another infant-size piece on her finger. "I think he does."

"Now how about you let me have a taste and see what I do?"

She spun around, the pie filling still clinging to her hand and found herself nose to nose with the man. "A...a taste?"

"Of pie." He slipped the plate away, moved to the counter and found the fork he had left lying there. "Don't worry, Josie. I won't press you for anything you're not ready to share. Not your secrets. Not your kisses. And most especially not your—"

Beep. Beep. Beep.

"What's that?"

"Bingo!"

"I didn't even know we were playing."

"Not the game, the mailman."

"We have a beeping mailman?"

"He has a little horn on his scooter to warn people to clear the path or let them know he's making a delivery. He has bad knees."

"When did Mt. Knott get a beeping mailman?"

"He's always been the mailman in this part of town as far as I know." She hurried across the room. "I can't believe you don't at least know about him. He certainly knows plenty about you."

"He does?"

Josie winced. She probably shouldn't have reminded him of how she had gotten people talking about Adam right after he came to town, which probably was how his father found out about Nathan, which led to the barbecue that Adam did not want to attend, which—

"So, who else have you talked to about me besides the bad-kneed beeper?"

"Bad-kneed beeper." Josie laughed. "I'll have to tell him that."

"Josie?"

She twisted the lock and pulled open the front door.

"Wouldn't have bothered you. I know you had big plans for today." Bingo eyed Adam.

Adam eyed him right back.

"But this looked important. Didn't want to take a chance of you not seeing it."

"He reads the mail?" Adam moved through the dining room in a few long strides. "You read her mail?"

"Just what's on the outside." The big man looked hurt and just a wee bit defensive. "Gotta read what's on the outside or else I wouldn't know what to deliver to where."

"Yeah, he's gotta read what's on the—" Josie turned the letter over and what was on the outside of the envelope hit her like a slap in the face. "It's the letter I sent to Ophelia to thank her for signing the papers to allow Nathan's adoption." Josie's hand trembled. "Marked 'Return to Sender.'"

"Really? I didn't know people actually did that." Adam moved in behind her, his hand out, but he did not try to take the envelope from her.

"Oh, yeah. All the time. Or they put 'not at the address.' The real creative ones sometimes send their own messages. Don't think I can say what they write on the envelopes, not in front of Josie." Bingo reached into his bag then and retrieved a stack of bills and advertising flyers. He thrust them toward her. "All means the same, the person on the address didn't get the mail."

She ignored the other mail and rubbed her fingertips over the blocky words beside her delicate-scrolled lettering. "Doesn't look like Ophelia's handwriting."

Adam took the mail from Bingo, his eyes always trained on her. "That good or bad?"

"Well, if it were in her own hand, I'd know she was there and just didn't, for whatever reason, want to hear from me." She looked up and blinked, half expecting tears to flood over her eyelashes, but they did not come.

"Family can be tough on each other." Adam brushed his hand over her shoulder.

"Some more than others," Bingo observed.

Adam smacked the mail in one hand against his open palm. "Don't you have mail to deliver?"

"Miss Josie?" Bingo looked to her to send him on his way.

She nodded.

"Now don't go fretting too much about that. Could be any number of things behind it, not all bad." He limped out the door, got onto his red scooter and gave a beep goodbye.

"You think that's true?" she asked Adam as they walked back to the counter. "That there are a lot of reasons mail gets returned and it doesn't mean that something bad has happened?"

"What do you think?"

"I think this means that Ophelia isn't at this address anymore."

"Then where is she?"

Where indeed? *You have a baby with her, why don't you know?* Josie pressed her lips together to keep her questions and quasi-accusations from exploding into the open. She rubbed the space between her eyebrows. At last she fought to keep from bursting into tears.

"Maybe you can contact your mother. She might know how to find Ophelia."

"She might. But in order to ask her, I'd have to first know where my *mother* is." That did it. The tears flowed, though less like a dam bursting and more in sobbing fits and starts.

Adam slapped the mail down and came to her. He started to touch her arms, then thought better of it. He tried to put his arm around her shoulders, but their shaking made that difficult. Finally he crooked one finger under her chin and lifted her face so he could look her in the eye as he said, "I don't understand."

"I haven't seen my mother since my grandmother's funeral." And at the mention of that, Josie felt completely and utterly alone all over again, just as she had the day of that funeral when her mother had driven off with her grandmother's car loaded down with anything of value from the house she and Josie had shared. "I spoke to her a time or two, but she called *me*. I don't have a number to call her. She stays on the move most of the time."

"On the move?" He dropped his hand and reached out to get a napkin from the dispenser on the counter. He handed it to her.

"Not running from the law or anything like that. At least not that I know of." She wiped her eyes, blew her nose, then grimaced. "Seems like Nathan might come by that tendency to stray from both sides of the family. You can't be too shocked by that, I mean, you and Ophelia…"

"I know." He hung his head. "I have no excuse for my behavior, Josie. I was hurt and angry and acting like a…a—"

"Like a toddler trying to get the people around him to stop everything and do his bidding?"

Adam chuckled softly at his own expense, then his expression went somber. He shook his head. "It was wrong. *I* was wrong. Doubly so to involve your sister. I didn't care that what we were doing would take its toll on her, the drinking, the carelessness of that temporary…relationship."

He struggled to get the words out without offending her, without embarrassing her.

For that Josie was grateful. And she showed it by trying to lift some of Adam's guilt. "You can't blame yourself for my sister. She was…*careless* and prone to the *temporary* for a long time before she met you."

"I know." He nodded. "She has her own pain. Her own deep-seated fears. Her own longing to make the people she loves notice her, to love her in return."

"Ophelia?" Josie had never thought of her sister that way.

Willful. Selfish. Haughty. Wild.

All of those things she had ascribed to the woman who shared her physical attributes but none of her spiritual convictions. But hurting? Fearful? Longing to be loved?

Josie had thought she alone had those feelings, that she alone deserved them. Had she really misjudged Ophelia so harshly?

The very notion rattled her to the core of her being.

"I never thought of her in that way. To me she was always Ophelia, the inspired. Ophelia, the nonconformist. Ophelia, Mom's favorite."

"Favorite?" Adam's whole expression clouded. "Burke said that about me today. Called me the favored son because I came back and because I gave my father a grandchild. But if you ask me there is no reason to favor me. I've handled so many things so poorly. The fact that Nathan is here and healthy, that's all you, Josie."

"Not *all* me," she spoke deliberately as the full measure of what her sister had done dawned on her. "Ophelia had Nathan. She carried him and chose not just to give him life but to give him a chance by bringing him to me and letting me care for him, be his mother."

"She knew you could do it."

Josie shook her head in awe. "That was a selfless act of pure faith, Adam. I never saw it until now. I never saw the real Ophelia until you showed her to me today."

"Me? I can barely see beyond the tip of my own nose, Josie."

"I don't believe that."

"How could you not? The whole time I've been in Mt. Knott I never once tried to find out about you and your family, just whined about my own."

"You've been so focused on your own issues… and rightly so. I'm nothing to you…"

"That's not true—about you being nothing to me, not about me being focused on my own issues. That, I hate to admit, is completely true." He took her by the arms and pulled her around so that he could look her in the eyes. "But I'm here now and I'm not going anywhere."

"Actually, I think you should."

"What?"

"Go," she said.

"But I—"

"Please, Adam. Just give me some time to myself. I have a lot to think about *and* a lot to do."

"I wanted to help you."

"If you want to help me, then pray for me."

"Okay."

"And for Nathan," she called as she watched him make his way to the door.

"Of course."

"And…" She folded her hands together, knowing she had to say one more thing and yet selfishly wishing she could just leave things as they were. To ask Adam to make his priorities that simple, her and Nathan.

But now she knew there was another person out there who needed God's love and compassion. And nothing would ever be right in their family until they faced that. "And pray for Ophelia, too."

Chapter Twelve

"You're too young to know this, Nathan, but there is an old saying. 'Today is the first day of the rest of your life.'" Josie lifted the baby from his crib.

She'd gotten up early. Even after staying up late into the night baking, she'd been too excited to sleep in. "This is not just the first day of the rest of my life. Except for the day that I knew for sure that I was going to be your momma, this is going to be the *best* day of the rest of my life."

She'd made up her mind about that as she'd baked and prayed and baked and prayed some more. The more she put her situation before the Lord—Ophelia, their mother, her feelings for Adam—the more she had come to appreciate the promise of the future. And that future started with this wonderful day.

"Dada."

"Yeah. Dada is going to be there right alongside

you and me at the family barbecue. And for the first time ever I am going to be part of a family."

Her whole life she'd wanted this. She'd dreamed of it. She'd prayed for it. Now, if only for a few sunny hours, she would know what that felt like.

"A family. I know I've always told you how everyone in this town, all the members of our church and all my customers who so kindly keep us in their prayers are our family, but it's not the same."

"Ya-ya-ya."

"And who knows? Maybe after the Burdetts see the community the way I do, they will see that the Crumble and the Crumble Pattie are a part of *our* family as well. And together we can…" Josie raised her head half expecting to hear fife-and-drum music playing the "Battle Hymn of the Republic" or some such patriotic and inspiring tune to accompany her homage to the power of people all working for a common good. Instead she saw her baby happily making spit bubbles and motor noises.

She sighed.

"It could happen. Especially with Adam back in town and you here to stay. Those both seem like reasons enough to make it work."

"Ya-ya-ya."

"And then with everyone working again, my business will pick up and I'll have enough money to finish up the adoption once and for all. *All* being me—" she poked him in the tummy to make him giggle "—you. Our own little family."

"Dada."

"And Dad, too, but not exactly…that is…" Josie considered not saying anymore about it.

Nathan didn't understand, after all, and she had started the day out in such a great frame of mind. Why muddy things up trying to wade through the complexities of their family dynamic?

One day Nathan would be old enough to understand and she needed to have practiced this speech often enough that she did not botch it up when it counted the most. "Okay, here's the deal, sweetheart. I have no idea what the deal is."

Nathan laughed.

Josie exhaled, her shoulders slumping forward. If she were Nathan's birth mother, if she were Ophelia, it would be different. Not easier, she realized, thinking back to the day before and her newfound empathy for her sister's situation. If she were Ophelia, she would still have to account for her behavior.

Josie might be well on her way to a new understanding of her sister, but Ophelia still had to be accountable for her past and for the things she had done to bring Nathan into the world. Among other things, she'd have to explain to her son about not being married and about keeping Nathan's existence a secret from his own natural father.

But from the legal end of things, if Josie *were* Nathan's birth mother, there wouldn't be lawyer fees and court costs to worry about. Unless Adam or his family had wanted to fight her for custody.

"If I were your birth mother, things wouldn't really be easier, would they?" She kissed her son's cheek. "They might be cheaper, but I can't even say that for sure. The only thing that would be different would be that I would know that Adam was not confusing his emotions for me with his emotions for the mother of his child, because I'd be both! But as things stand now, I have no idea how to know if he really cares about me, or—"

Ding-dong.

"Pack mule at your service!" Adam nudged the front door and presented himself for her inspection.

He wore jeans with holes in the knees. Sported a faded orange-and-blue T-shirt with the old Carolina Crumble Pattie logo on it from back in the days when they had enough workers to sponsor a softball team. And squashing down his dark, gorgeous hair was a bright-green John Deere baseball cap.

"I want you to know I don't do this for just anybody," he said.

"Do? Do what?" She tried not to laugh outright. "Dress up like a scarecrow?"

"Haul pies. I mean it, Josie, not only am I going to a place I had wanted to avoid, and to spend time with people I had wanted to ignore, I got up early on a Saturday morning to take *pastry* to a *bakery*. If that's not a sign of blind devotion, then I don't know what is."

"Blind devotion? Well, that certainly explains the way you're dressed. No one with 20/20 vision could have put that outfit together."

"I think I look adorable. What do you think, son?"

"Dada." A squeal. More spit bubbles. A laugh.

"I have half a mind—"

Josie opened her mouth to second that, jokingly.

He held one finger up to silence her. "Half a mind, but a full heart."

She sank her teeth into her bottom lip to let him know she wasn't going to try to best that.

"Half a mind, full heart and an empty bakery truck. All of them at your disposal."

Were his mind and heart really hers? Josie didn't dare dwell on that question. So she asked about the safest offering. "A bakery truck?"

"Unless you have a better idea for how to transport to the Crumble enough pie to feed all of Mt. Knott."

Josie went to the door and peered out at the truck usually seen making deliveries throughout the county, including the occasional, stealthy stop at Josie's Home Cookin' Kitchen.

"I had Jed and Warren and some moms in minivans each going to take as many pies as they thought they could safely transport."

"Jed and Warren? When you counted how many pies they could 'safely' transport I hope you allowed for the ones that would not be 'safe' in their hands." He smiled.

Josie smiled, too. She actually had planned on having a pie or two go missing during the short trip to the Crumble. Josie smiled because Adam had thought of it, too. For a guy who had only just returned to a town he purported to have held in contempt, he sure had gotten a feel for—and a good-natured regard for—the locals awfully fast.

That spoke well of the man, she thought. As someone who had moved often and under questionable circumstances, Josie had learned that often what you got out of new relationships was directly proportionate to what you put into them. That is, if you bothered to put anything into them at all. Adam *had* bothered.

Not only that, he had made connections. Clearly, he liked Warren and Jed, and they liked him. She just knew that if Adam gave everyone in Mt. Knott the same chance, they would have the same results. And then...

The rabbit-fast thumping of her heart made her nip any kind of further speculation in the bud. She narrowed her eyes at the bakery truck Adam had so sweetly put at her disposal.

"It's not an elegant horse charging to your rescue, but then I'm more black sheep than white knight." He gave a shallow bow followed by a brazen wink.

Sheep. Not stray dog. Josie tried not to read too much into that, but given their talk about the Lord as a shepherd and what it meant to bring the lost lambs home, she couldn't help but stare at the old truck and murmur, "This is better. This is much better."

On sheer impulse she went up on tiptoe and kissed his cheek.

"Much better," he murmured, his dark eyes glittering as she stood with her face just inches from his. "Much, much better."

"Much, much," she whispered, lost in his eyes, not exactly sure what she had just agreed with.

He gave her an answer by returning her kiss—right on the front porch where everyone in Mt. Knott could see.

And Josie didn't care.

The kiss was sweet and brief, but it took Josie's breath away and left her knees wobbling. Just the way a real first kiss was supposed to.

When it ended she realized she had her hands on Adam's shoulders. She jerked them away as if he had suddenly become hot to her touch.

He snagged her by the wrist. "Josie, I, this…this has all happened so fast for me."

"Me, too."

"Yeah, I know but you've had a little more time to get used to some of it. Suddenly I'm a father, or at least I have a child."

"Da-da-da." Nathan, who had been cruising around the furniture in the living room while his parents stood in the open doorway, dropped down and banged a spoon on the floor.

"You're a father," she assured him.

"And I'm back in Mt. Knott."

"Believe me, I've noticed that."

"And suddenly my family is having this big shin-dig in my honor." He scoffed at the last word to show he felt he either did not have any honor or did not deserve for his family to treat him with it.

"It will be fun, just wait and see."

"I've never been any good at waiting," he said, stepping close.

"Think of yourself as setting a good example for your son."

"You've used that on me before."

"Parenting is a job that knows no hours and never ends. Nathan learns from us all the time. We don't just teach him through our words but also through our actions."

"Is that your way of saying I shouldn't grab you up and kiss you on the spot."

"On *this* spot," she touched her cheek. "That's okay, I suppose. For anything else, I think we'd better wait until after the barbecue when we can be alone to talk things through."

"What if you don't feel like talking to—or kissing—me after the barbecue?"

"Why wouldn't I?"

"I don't know."

Josie's stomach tightened just a little. All these things she had been thinking of Adam, had she just come up with them because she wanted them so badly to be true? She had lived in dreams—dreams of being in a family, of having a family, of having a real home—had she lost track of the harsh realities surrounding this man?

She looked deep into his eyes.

Naw. What she saw there was no fantasy.

She shook her head. "Sometimes I think you take this man-of-mystery persona a little too seriously, Adam."

"Me? A mystery? Why, I'm the easiest guy in the world to figure out."

Josie sputtered out a laugh.

"I'm just a man who isn't afraid to ask for what he wants."

"Like you asked for your inheritance for example?"

"I was thinking more like asking for another kiss."

She wagged her finger at him and shook her head. "Asking for what you want might work when you're asking for a kiss that doesn't mean anything. But when you ask for a kiss from *me,* and especially in our situation, I think you had better *ask* if you want everything that comes with it."

"I'm…I'm not completely certain what that is."

Josie raised an eyebrow. "Oh?"

"Look, Josie, I don't know exactly what will happen between us after today. That's just flat-out reality. I do know that I would very much like for there to be an 'after today' for the two of us, however."

"That's part of the problem, Adam. There is no 'two of us.'"

"Not yet." He inched closer still.

"Not ever." She gave him a light but firm shove. "There will never just be the two of us. We have Nathan to think of."

"I don't see how our having a good relationship can be a bad thing for Nathan."

"It's not, *if* we have a *good* relationship, a solid one. Those can't be built on shaky ground."

"Then we may be in trouble, because every time I'm near you the earth moves and I can hardly keep my footing." He grinned.

"We have not known each other long enough for you to make a judgment like that," she warned, even though she felt exactly the same way.

"Haven't we? I feel as if I've known you a long time."

"But you haven't." She held her breath a moment and considered holding back her opinion about what Adam was experiencing. But she couldn't. He had kissed her once already and awakened all sorts of doubts in her. If they ever hoped to work through her apprehensions, they had to deal with them out in the open. "Are you sure you don't have me confused with someone you have known longer and with much more intimacy?"

"You mean Ophelia?"

"Of course I mean Ophelia. I *am* her identical twin."

"Her twin, sure, but identical? Not by a long shot."

"We have the same build, basically. The same hair

color, complexion and face. I suspect if you saw us together you wouldn't be able to tell us apart."

"Oh, yes I would. You two may *look* alike. That doesn't mean you are alike."

"Of course not. But given the short time you've known either of us…" She let him draw his own conclusions.

"I realized who you were once I saw you holding my son, Josie. Protecting him. You are his mother." Adam brushed her hair back. He bent in close, but instead of trying to kiss her lips, he planted a kiss on her forehead. "And I can't thank you enough for that."

"Really?"

"And for the record I know the difference between you and your sister. I know you, Josie. I don't know Ophelia. I'm ashamed to have to admit it but I never really knew her, any more than I think she knew me. That's one of those things people who ridicule Christian values never get around to mentioning when they make it seem that satisfying every animal urge is normal and healthy."

"What?"

"They don't tell you how lonely that kind of encounter can leave you, how empty. How like a wounded animal, a—"

"A stray?"

He nodded.

"I know you are applying that to Ophelia, Adam,

but you might want to take a look at how it applies to your family."

"My family?"

"Sure. You give in to the easy urge to feel sorry for yourself. To snap at the people you had to rely upon, to foster distrust of them. Those are not the acts of a man who is trying to live like Christ."

It took him a moment and a few long, slow breaths, but finally he closed his eyes and nodded. "I see your point."

"Now as to you and Ophelia—"

"There is no me and Ophelia. Despite Nathan as evidence to the contrary, there never was, really."

"I wish that made me feel better, Adam." She retreated inside, went to her son and picked him up. "Relationships and parenting are hard enough without having to cope with this kind of thing."

"This kind of thing? You mean the whole identical-twins, secret-baby-of-prominent-local-lineage, fathered-by-returning-ne'er-do-well-son thing?" Adam followed her inside, chuckling. "You actually know other people who have to cope with *that* in their relationships?"

"Well-l-l-l." Josie rocked from side to side with Nathan on her hip before rolling her eyes and conceding with a shy laugh. "Well, no relationship is perfect!"

"I guess not." Adam laughed, too. "So, how do you suppose that, year after year, generation after generation of imperfect people have managed to fall in love, make a commitment, establish homes, raise families and grow old together?"

Josie fell very quiet. "A lot of them haven't managed those things."

"But those who have, what do you suppose a lot of them relied upon to help them get through it all?"

"God," she said softly.

"Then let's me and you do that, too, Josie." Adam held his hand out to her.

"You want…to *pray*…with me?"

"It surprises me a little, too, but these past few days I've thought a lot about my new role and what I need to do, about businesses based on Biblical principles and…about us. I think it's the right thing to do, don't you?"

She did. So she slipped her hand into his.

Adam took her hand and bowed his head. For a long moment he said nothing. Or perhaps he prayed in silence. Josie didn't know exactly what to do, so she used the moment to gather her thoughts, to humble herself before the Lord and to praise him and thank him.

She had so much to be grateful for, she realized, even in the midst of all her doubts. For Nathan. For Mt. Knott. For her work. For her baking talent. For Adam.

And for this day. This chance to know how it felt to be a part of a real family.

She drew a deep breath and held it. That's when she realized that Adam had begun to speak.

"I am a lost sheep, Lord, returned to the fold, and

yet not even sure he belongs *in* that fold. I did not come in humility and hope, but bearing pride and a grudge. I am flawed and fearful that I am unfit for the task You have set before me, to be a father to Nathan and a friend to Josie."

"Friend," she whispered before she could stop herself.

"Because of all the demands on any relationship, but most of all of those between a man and a woman raising a child together, the bonds of friendship are necessary to endure one another's faults and missteps with laughter and good will. Thank You for bringing Josie into my life and into the life of our son, Nathan. Help us to face this and every day with faith in You and trust in each other."

He squeezed her hand, which Josie recognized as his way of asking her if she had something to add.

"Bless all those who gather today." She choked back her emotions. So many things she wanted to say. So many things she simply could not express except to say, "We submit to Your will and praise Your holy name."

"Amen," Adam murmured.

"Amen," Josie agreed.

He released one of her hands but clung to the other long enough to coax her to look up and meet his gaze.

"You ready for this?"

For what? she wanted to ask. *For you and I to begin our "friendship"? Or for the responsibility of*

transporting and serving enough pie to fill up the
considerable bellies of every hungry person in Mt.
Knott?

"I'm, uh, I'm not sure."

"Neither am I." He laughed softly, almost not a
laugh at all. "But ready or not, here we go."

Chapter Thirteen

Adam would have loved more time alone with Josie, but knew it was for the best that Jed and Warren showed up honking their horns and hollering to their "Sweetie Pie" that they had come to fill up their trucks. Of course, as soon as they peered inside the bakery truck they agreed it was a much better mode of pie transportation.

They happily helped Adam load up the supplies while Josie ran around with the phone glued to her ear, frantically reorganizing her moms-with-mini-vans, answering last-minute questions and checking on the lopsided status of salads versus sides. And each time the three men saw her, she had on a different outfit.

Finally one of the moms arrived in her triple-car-seat and double-bumper-sticker brand-new minivan. With much persuasion she loaded up Nathan and pledged to look after him until Josie and Adam got there.

Josie waved goodbye to the happy toddler, then rushed inside her house, shouting as she did, "I'll be ready in a sec, Adam. Just let me get a change of clothes."

"You have a whole pile of clothes that you've changed into and out of already on your bedroom floor," Adam reminded her.

"I know, but I just remembered something I have in the back of my closet," she called back.

"You look—"

Warren cut him off with a somber shake of his head. "Don't even try to finish that sentence, son. Not if you hope to get rolling toward the Crumble in the next twenty minutes."

Jed stood on the front-porch steps. "Warren's right."

Warren cupped his hand to his ear and grinned. "Say that again."

"On this *one* occasion." Jed drove home the point by placing his hand alongside his mouth and shouting it for all to hear, before he dropped both the hand and his voice and grumbled, "Warren is right."

Warren chuckled, then turned to Adam, motioning for him to follow along as the older men went to their trucks. "It's one of them, what you call, no-win situations."

"A trap." Jed nodded.

Adam paused on the lawn. "A trap?"

"Uh-huh. Not a bear-trap type of thing, though. More one of those woven-finger-puzzle deals." Jed touched the ends of both his index fingers together and Adam could picture exactly what he was talking about.

"If you start trying to reason with a woman about how she looks in some kind of outfit you will never be able to extricate yourself."

Adam thought of the red-white-and-blue shirt that looked sort of sailorish, and the white jeans she had been wearing. "I was just going to say she looks fine."

Jed sucked air between his teeth.

Warren winced. "Fine? You actually intended to use that word? Fine?"

"But she does. She looks—"

"Shhhh." Jed put his finger to his lips.

"Don't say it again." Warren opened the driver's-side door on his sun-faded blue truck. He hopped in and gunned the engine. "We'll meet you down at the Home Cookin' Kitchen to help load up the pies."

Jed got into his green truck and gave a wave. "You can thank us later."

Adam didn't know if the men meant he should thank them for stopping him from getting into a no-win situation with Josie or for loading the pies. Either way it made him a bit uneasy to feel he was in any man's debt.

That thought kept him quiet on the whole trip to Josie's Home Cookin' Kitchen to collect the baked goods, and as he and the other men passed one another taking pie after pie to the big, waiting bakery truck.

He had come back to Mt. Knott to square away old

debts, as it were, to tie up loose ends and be done with the place once and for all. He stood on the sidewalk and watched the comings and goings of Josie's friends and neighbors, so happy to pitch in and make this barbecue a success for everyone involved.

Mt. Knott, he decided, was not a place you could just be done with all that easily. Each new day, each new association, brought with it a responsibility to others, a connection, an opportunity to be a part of something good and productive and hopeful. How had he lived here so long and not seen that? How had he worked among these people and still managed to lose his way?

He only had to think of the benefactor of today's picnic to find the answer to that question. Adam set his jaw. As soon as they finished loading the pies he would be going out to the Crumble for the biggest showdown of his life so far. He would face his father, not as a black sheep or somebody else's baby, but as an equal. Or perhaps, depending on Dora's recommendation, as his boss.

Why didn't Adam feel better about that?

"That's the last of them." Jed slapped Adam on the back. "You be careful with that precious cargo now, you hear?"

"Don't worry." Adam shook off the sting between his shoulder blades. "Not a single piece of crust will be broken."

"I ain't worried about the pie, you just get our girl there in one piece."

"Okay, let's do this." Josie stood before him, all smiles and softness.

Something was different about her, but he couldn't put his finger on it. Of course, if he tried to put his finger on anything to do with Josie, Adam knew she'd slap it away and tell him what for. He smiled at the thought and hurried to open the door of the bakery truck for her.

"Thank you." She bowed her head, started to climb in, then stepped back and asked, "By the way, how do I look?"

It's a trap. He could hear Jed growling out a warning.

A no-win situation. And Warren, too.

Adam shut his eyes and kissed her so lightly on the temple that he wasn't sure he hadn't simply kissed a wayward curl. Then he whispered, "You always look perfect to me, Josie."

"That's so sweet." She glanced a feather-light kiss of her own off his jaw then got into the truck. "Let's go out to the Crumble, then."

The Crumble. How many times had Adam snickered cynically over the aptness of that tag for the place he intended to bring down once and for all? Now it sounded like one of the sweetest places on earth.

He drove down the town's tree-lined street waving as he did to the people bustling out to their cars. They carried blankets and baskets, folding chairs and portable playpens, outdoor games for the kids and at least one wheelchair for an elderly member of the family. This was a big day in Mt. Knott. The Burdetts were finally giving something back, and no one wanted to be left out.

He rolled through the streets of Mt. Knott, past the post office with the American flag—the largest of many that hung from the handful of businesses still operating in the old downtown area—fluttering overhead.

Bingo pulled up on the sidewalk alongside Adam's truck, waved from his scooter and hollered out, "I'll be out to the Crumble soon as I finish up my route. Don't let Jed and Warren eat all the choice cuts and leave me with nothing but bones and gristle!"

"Jed and Warren *are* nothing but bones and gristle," Adam joked. Still, he hated to think about the kind of trouble he'd bring down on himself if he actually tried to get between Josie's best patrons and the buffet table. "So you'd better kick that scooter into high gear and don't waste any time getting out there yourself."

"Will do!" Bingo gave a salute with the packet of mail in his hand then, true to his word, zoomed off down the sidewalk at top speed leaving Adam in his proverbial dust.

"Admit it."

"What?" Adam scowled.

"This place is starting to get to you."

"What? I've lived in Mt. Knott all my life."

"No, you never lived in Mt. Knott, not really. And

now that you've got a taste of it, it's gotten to you. You're starting to care about these people."

"Some more than others," he said almost under his breath.

She leaned back against the gray-and-brown upholstery and looked out the side window. "I'll tell Bingo you said so."

Adam barked out a laugh.

Josie shifted her shoulders so that her upper body faced him, and she smiled, clearly pleased with herself.

But over what? The joke or because she thought she had him figured out? Had the people of Mt. Knott "gotten" to him all that much? How could that be when he had known them, or known of them, or known they existed at least, all his life? "I want to go on record as not accepting that I haven't lived in Mt. Knott all my life. Except for college I've been right here."

"You have that right. You said so yourself, you spent most of your life right here." She made an open-handed gesture toward the slightly rusted sign proclaiming, Carolina Crumble Pattie Way. "On this road, at the Crumble or at the big ol' Burdett mansion."

"It's hardly a mansion."

"Compared to most of the houses around town?" She waved at some kids who had twisted around and were making faces from the back window of the car in front of them. "It's a mansion."

He tucked his chin down and squinted at her a bit sideways, so as not to take his eyes completely off the road. "You've been there?"

"Well, no. I just always *imagined.*"

"It's not a mansion," he insisted. "It's a home. *My home.*"

He had never thought of it that way, not even as a kid, but suddenly it was the only way he could see the large craftsman-style residence with secondary ranch- and cottage-style houses for the brothers on adjoining lots. *Home.*

Josie had never been there, and he wanted to take her.

"It's more of a compound, actually. You know, a big piece of land with one big house and some smaller ones. Burke has a ranch-style. Jason has a smaller version of the big house. Cody and Carol have a bungalow, or, uh, is it a cottage? Do you know the difference?"

She shook her head.

"Neither do I," he admitted.

"And where did you live when you were out there? The barn?"

Actually he had a log house. Strong and sturdy and set apart from the rest, but lacking anything to make it personal inside, anything to give him a reason to have gone there to stay or even visit on this trip back. "Yeah. Me and the other lost sheep, we bunked out in the barn. Baaa-aaah."

"Except you're not lost anymore," she reminded him. "You found your way home."

Adam started to refute that, or maybe ask Josie what role she had played in bringing it about, but just then he realized they were at their destination.

"Stop." She held her hand up flat. "I'm going to get out and go on ahead. See that big white tent over there?"

"Sure." How could he miss it?

"You make your way to that and I'll figure out the best place for you to park to unload."

"Can't you just ride over with me?"

She frowned at the slowly moving line of cars ahead of them. "Adam, I'm supposed to be in charge here. I can't do that from the back of the crowd."

"Okay."

"See you in a minute." And out she got.

Cautiously he made his way through the old rutted parking lot toward the open area where the barbecue would be held. Partly because he didn't want to arrive with a single one of Josie's pies damaged and partly because he wanted to savor every moment leading up to…

Well, that was it, wasn't it? He had no real idea what he was going to find at the Crumble. No idea what recommendation Dora might have for him. No idea how his brothers would react to his suddenly showing up. No explanation for how his father could be so welcoming to him after a lifetime of treating

Adam like an outsider and then more than a year of Adam *behaving* like an outsider.

Josie's warning to know what he wanted rang in his ears.

When he had arrived in Mt. Knott he thought he'd had such clear goals. He had planned everything, step by step. First step, get out from under his family once and for all. Second step, make anyone who had wronged him pay for not accepting him, not believing in him, by taking over the Crumble and making everyone accountable to him. Third step...

He really hadn't gotten beyond the second step. Two steps then nothing? Now *there* was a surefire way to get nowhere.

He supposed he could still make a run for it.

Then he saw Josie with the baby in her arms, standing by the large white tent.

The instant she saw him, her face lit up. With her hair that wild knot of curls, her cheeks red and a crowd surrounding her demanding her attention, she looked frazzled but happy. She pointed to a parking spot just the right size for the bakery truck and gave a weary but grateful smile.

Adam wasn't going anywhere but right where she needed him to be.

He parked, hopped out of the truck and went straight to her.

It was perfect outside, as if the weather itself were connected to the mood in Adam's heart. Bright and sunny, but not blazing. Breezy enough to keep the bugs away but not strong enough to fan barbecue smoke into everyone's eyes and effect the taste of all the food.

And Josie looked perfect, as well. Fair as the day and just as gentle, but with just enough energy and bluster to keep him on his toes. Adam reached out and took Nathan from her, bending as he did to place a kiss on her cheek. It seemed the most natural thing in the world. His way of both thanking her for doing all this and of reassuring her that he would be there for her should it start to overwhelm her.

It wasn't until he heard the subtle gasps and chuckles from the crowd around them that he realized the larger implications of what he'd done.

"What?" He looked around them, challenge in his tone, his posture and his words. "Just my way of thanking Josie for doing such a good job with the pies and all."

"Oh? Is that how it's done?" Jed moseyed up to the forefront with Warren at his side. "Here me and Warren been rubbing our bellies, saying 'Mmm-Mmm' and leaving generous tips when we pay our bills."

"Didn't know we could accomplish as much with a Yankee dime."

Adam scowled at the old expression. The way he understood it a Yankee dime was a stolen kiss that meant nothing to the one doing the kissing. He didn't like the implication. A week ago he'd have glared at the old guys and told them just what he thought.

A week ago he'd been a "Stray Dawg" who had both bark and bite. Now?

Now he knew how to play the game.

"Hey, I was just following orders." He raised his shoulders and dropped them.

"Someone give you orders to go slopping sugar on our Sweetie Pie?" Warren studied the crowd as if the guilty party might just step forward and save him the trouble of having to sniff him out.

"Yeah." Adam folded his arms over his chest. "You did."

"Me?"

"You told me to take special care of my precious cargo. I did just that. And here she is, signed, sealed and delivered."

"You said that, Warren?"

And if he needed more proof that he was, indeed, a stray in this town no longer, Adam brought the joke home. "He did. But then he also said that I shouldn't tell you that you look fi-*i*-ne in that outfit."

It wasn't a lie. But Adam did feel a twinge of guilt that drawing out the word *fine* like that did give it a bit of a different spin, implying he thought she looked great instead of merely suitable.

"You don't like this outfit?" She turned on Warren.

"No. I never said—"

"No?" She pulled out the fluff of pink holding her hair up on top of her head. "I knew I shouldn't have changed out of the patriotic one."

"No, I meant yes."

"Trap," Jed muttered.

"Yes?" Josie worked her fingers through her hair trying to get it to…well, no telling what she wanted it to do. What it *was* doing was falling around her shoulders and sticking to her cheeks. "Yes what? That I should have changed?"

"No." Warren shot Adam a look that would have melted butter.

It didn't affect Adam, of course, especially when he caught a glimpse of a short black haircut darting through the clusters of picnickers at Dora Hoag speed. "If y'all will excuse me, I'll be right back."

With that he took off after the woman, trying his best not to appear to have just taken off after anyone, least of all a woman. Didn't want to give the town anything to gab about tonight over pie.

He glanced back over his shoulder at Josie, who kept bobbing up and down on her toes, trying to peer over people to find him.

Correction. He didn't want to give the town anything *else* to gab about over pie and coffee tonight.

"Ms. Hoag?" Somehow he managed to shout out her name without getting his voice beyond a stage whisper.

It must have worked because the woman whirled around just as he came up to her and practically jumped out of her skin. "Burdett. You're here."

"Of course I'm here. I'm the guest of, um, honor."

"Not to hear your brother tell it." She smiled slow and sly.

Adam had no idea his boss was capable of that kind of smile, or of making a joke. Or dressing as if she truly belonged at a Carolina barbecue. "You look, uh…"

"Hold the small talk, Burdett." She flashed her palm outward to keep him from making a fool of himself trying to keep his compliment businesslike. "I know what you want."

"You do?" Adam snorted out a hard laugh. "Wish you had told me that months ago. Would have saved me a whole world of heartache."

"What? I don't…"

Adam dropped the jest and became all business again. "You're talking about your recommendation, of course."

"Yes, I've… I've gone over the preliminaries and—"

"Maybe we should go somewhere more private for this." He looked around them. They stood in the shade of a tree that Adam had remembered being big enough for climbing even when he was a kid. It was huge now, but somehow it seemed smaller than it did back then. And while it offered cool, pleasant shade, the soothing rustle of thick leaves and the smell of earth and bark mingled with the tangy smoke from the barbecue, it also seemed too casual a place to hear this kind of news. Besides, between the tree and the passing knots of family and friends, it seemed too out in the open. A place where they could be too easily spotted, too easily overheard.

"We don't need to go anywhere."

"But—"

"Because I am meeting your brother here any minute and because there is nowhere on these grounds that are going to make this any easier to say."

Adam's heart leaped. What was the expression, one man's trash is another man's treasure? Dora Hoag thought she was delivering bad news but that "bad news" was exactly what Adam had been hoping for. "You are going to recommend Global pass on the Carolina Crumble Pattie, lock, stock and lousy building."

"Just the opposite."

Adam froze halfway to high-fiving his very proper boss. "What?"

"I am going to recommend that Global buy the Carolina Crumble Pattie lock, stock and lousy building. Then tear it down."

"Tear it…what?"

"Down. To the ground." She jabbed one finger in the direction of the roots of the old tree. "Take the recipe and put it in a vault and leave it there while we try to come up with a cost-effective alternative. And in a few years, when people get nostalgic for the old snack cake, we will bring it back with a fanfare and sell it internationally."

"Cost effective? Meaning inferior?"

"We can't go on using the best ingredients, Burdett. If we did, we'd have to charge as much for a single patty as we normally charge for a whole box of snack cakes."

"Have you ever tasted a Carolina Crumble Pattie? They are worth a dozen boxes of those flavorless globs of chemicals Wholesome Hearth calls snacks."

"I know." She shifted her feet, twisted her hands together, then craned her neck, all signs she wished Burke would show up and rescue her from having to talk to Adam about this. "That's why I'm saying we have to vault the recipe and give it some time before we come out with our version."

"Under the Carolina Crumble Pattie name?" Adam kept his gaze trained in hers even though out of the corner of his eyes he could see his oldest brother approaching.

"Of course. We need to own the name. It has thirty years of great marketing behind it."

"It has a lot more than marketing behind it, and that's the part you can't buy or keep in a vault."

"A family's life work? A product made with care, the pride of a whole community? A standard of excellence?"

"And more," Adam said.

"We don't want those things." Dora batted her eyes and waved her hand. "We just want the perception of having those things. And that's what we get by buying your family out and using their reputation and product branding."

Adam sighed. He'd been through this before with other products and had always convinced himself that, as Dora had often reminded him, it wasn't personal.

But this? This *was* personal. "What about modernizing the facilities? Adding new snack lines? Giving stock to employees? Given enough time, work and money, I could make the Carolina Crumble Pattie an international moneymaker."

"Of that I have no doubt."

"But?"

"But you don't work for Carolina Crumble Pattie, Burdett. You work for the Wholesome Hearth Country Fresh Bakery."

"I'd gladly step down and take on a different position in order to oversee this project."

"You would?" She tipped her head to one side, clearly not sure what to make of that.

"You would?" Burke rounded the old tree. His tone was far more disbelieving than that of Adam's boss.

"Yes, I would." Even Adam hadn't known he was going to say that until it was out of his mouth. But now that it was out there… "Gladly."

Dora acknowledged Burke's arrival with nothing more than a shift of her head. Her focus remained on Adam. "That's all well and good and perhaps even leans slightly to the noble, Burdett."

"Thank you." Adam puffed his chest up a bit.

She put her hands on her slender hips. "But we don't need nobility at Global."

"What?" He exhaled and leaned against the tree.

"We need you. We need your sharklike instincts. We need you to ferret out small places like this so we can move in and do whatever we have to do to help keep Wholesome Hearth at the top of Global's international food chain."

Adam replayed that message in his head once, then twice, each time gleaning new bits of information that led him to conclude, "First I'm a shark. Then I'm a weasel. Finally I'm just something at the bottom of the food chain?"

"Up to you." Dora shrugged. "You can be whoever you want to be."

Be whoever he wanted to be? In his whole life no one had ever believed that of him.

From somewhere in the crowd he heard Josie's laughter.

His whole life no one had ever believed he could be whoever he wanted to be: that he could be more than a stray dog; that he could be a better Christian; a better businessman; a better citizen; and Nathan's daddy.

Except...

"There's just one thing I have to ask you, Dora."

She arched a pencil-thin eyebrow, though Adam didn't know if the subtle but slightly spooky affectation was in reaction to his demand to ask her something or to his using her first name so casually.

"I'm listening," she said, finally.

"When we first came out here, you said business is nothing personal."

"Uh-huh."

"But then you also let it be known that you didn't think it wasn't such a bad thing for a business to be based on Biblical principles."

"I don't know what you're getting at."

"I want to know which method you used to arrive at your recommendation? The nothing personal or the Biblical?"

She smiled slowly. "I did what Global pays me to do."

"And Global was founded on Biblical principles?"

"*Was* founded. Global has changed."

He thought as much. If she had said she had come to this decision through prayer and an understanding of guiding principles, he would have needed to hear more. But given this information, he knew what he had to say and what he had to do. "Global *has* changed. But then, so have I."

"Which means?"

"I quit."

Chapter Fourteen

"You what?" Josie tried to make the words Adam had just spoken make sense.

"Quit."

"Quit what?" She darted her gaze to the people and things surrounding them. "Quit your family? Quit the barbecue? Quit…on me?"

"No. No." He took her by the upper arms and bent slightly to put them in a direct line of vision. "I would never quit on you, Josie."

"Then…?"

"I quit my job."

"Your factory job?"

"My…" He didn't have to say another word for Josie to know how wrong the speculation that he had blown his inheritance and had to take a job in a rival food factory.

"You don't have a factory job, do you?"

"Not unless Global moved the office of vice president of acquisitions and mergers for Wholesome Hearth Country Fresh Bakery into the factory, no, I don't."

"Vice President?"

"It's not as big a deal as you might think. Global has VPs by the dozens."

"But now they have one less?"

"Yeah. Now they have one less." He practically beamed with the news.

"Why?"

"Because I just quit."

"Why did you quit?"

"Oh." His whole expression fell.

Josie had been too busy to eat today and yet she suddenly felt as if her stomach was filled with stones. "Adam?"

He groaned and rubbed the bridge of his nose with his thumb and forefinger. He scrunched his eyes shut tight. His usually smooth skin creased into faint crow's feet. His shoulders went rigid.

It made her think of the image Conner Burdett had spoken of, of the little boy with his hands perpetually in fists. She ventured a touch on his forearm, trying to encourage him to unclench and trust her, though she wasn't sure he would. He had never come to trust his father, why would she be any different. "Adam?"

"Josie, I've…I've kept so much from you."

"I've kept something from you, as well."

"What?"

"My secret ingredient." She knew it was not on the same scale. Whatever Adam had kept from her, and probably others in town and in his family, had led him to a point where he found relief and pride in having quit a very high-powered and fancy-titled job. She had said it, though, to try to lighten the mood. And, to try to shore up the connection between them, she quickly added, "Remember when you said you'd tell me your secret if I'd tell you mine?"

He dropped his hand to his side, and the creases in his face relaxed, just a little. He even managed a hint of a smile, but only a hint. And he looked as if it could thin out to a scowl without much provocation. "I remember."

"Well then, I'll make it easier for you to tell me what's going on with you." She curled her fingers into the soft fabric of his orange-and-blue striped baseball shirt and stepped close enough to shut the people around them out. "I'll tell you my secret ingredient, then you can tell me about your secret, um, life."

"Doesn't sound like a fair exchange." He gazed deeply into her eyes, his gratitude at the way she had taken all this evident.

"Are you kidding? You've tasted my pies. I've seen the mess you have made in your life. Who do you really think is getting the bigger secret here?" She laughed. It rang a bit hollow, but not phony. "Are you ready?"

"Anytime," he whispered.

"My secret ingredient is…"

She actually felt people inching close to them as she spoke those words. She gave them a backward glance, her eyes narrowed in warning.

Not a person retreated.

She cleared her throat and went up on tiptoe, cupping her hand to shield her mouth as she leaned close and whispered in Adam's ear. "I pulverize a Carolina Crumble Pattie into the mix for the top crust, then brush it with butter and my own mix of spices the last few minutes of browning."

Adam pulled back, his face a blank.

Suddenly Josie felt those stones she had imagined in her stomach grow ice cold and begin to tumble around.

"So if the Crumble closed…" Adam said.

"The Crumble is closing?" A man standing near them asked in a voice that carried across the gathering.

Adam shook his head. He held up his hand. "No!"

"Stray Dawg says the Crumble is closing," the man repeated louder this time.

"I knew his coming here was suspicious," Elvie chimed in straight away. "You know he works for a competitor, don't you? I heard he and his brother are in on this—courting an exec from Wholesome Hearth—"

"Please. Stop. Wait. Listen. Burke is not a part of this." Adam tried to take it back, to stop the remark from turning into a wild rumor that would spread like fire through the closely knit community.

And who knew who would get singed by the flames?

Josie could already feel the heat. "If the Crumble closes, Adam? You want to know what would happen to me? I'd not just be out of an ingredient, I would be out of my livelihood."

"Josie—"

The murmuring around them grew louder and louder.

"Belly-up and bankrupt because I'd have no way to pay back my small-business loan." Josie swallowed to keep the cold lump of fear from rising and strangling her. "So, you see, you have to do everything you can to make sure that does not happen."

"It's not. It won't." He gave her a shake and a look that said he meant that with all his heart. "Not if I can do anything to stop it, it won't."

"Those words would mean a bit more if you weren't the one that started the ball rolling on this whole thing." Adam's older brother loomed behind him, seeming to have shown up from out of nowhere.

"You? You are the one responsible for closing the Crumble?" Josie still could not make it all fit together. She searched Adam's face, but found no comfort in his pinched and pained expression.

"Ya-ya-ya." From a few feet away she heard her baby babbling. She whipped around to find him in

Jed's arms, blissfully alternating between chewing on a cookie and slobbering on Jed's shirt. The older man didn't even seem to notice as he smiled at her and nodded.

Warren stood beside him, and Warren's wife. She took her husband's hand and all of them smiled at her as if to tell her that they were there to support her no matter what.

That's when it hit Josie. No matter what happened with the factory or the town, she had the thing she had always wished for. She had a family. Not in the conventional sense but a very real one nonetheless. She had people who cared for her and her son. She had a place to go in a time of need. She had the love of the Lord and she had hope. She always had hope.

"The Crumble is not closing," Adam said, drawing her attention back to him.

"You don't have any say in that anymore," Burke reminded his brother.

"Stray Dawg is the one closing the place down," Elvie announced to the people who had shown up late.

"I knowed there was something sneaky about his coming back to town," one of the newcomers yelled.

"Don't go talking about my big brother Adam like that." Jason, Lucky Dawg, came forward and took his place beside Burke. "He's not sneaky. He's right here in the open."

"Would everybody calm down here? This is all rumor and speculation. Nothing productive can come from that." Cody joined his other brothers, hand in hand with his wife, Carol. "Now, I know all of you folks and I minister to a good deal of you. I'm not saying you don't have a right to your feelings. I'm just here to say that Adam is not just my brother but he's yours as well. A brother in the Lord. We need to think about that before we go throwing stones."

"If the Crumble does close, I want you all to know, it won't be my doing." Adam snagged Josie by the wrist. "I did not foresee this. I did not want it."

"You still don't get it, do you?" Burke planted his feet shoulder-width apart and crossed his arms. His very stance spoke of holding his ground and challenging his brother. "You think Dad is throwing you this shindig because he suddenly cares about all these people? Because you coming back made him a new man and helped him see the error of his ways?"

"I, uh…" Adam glanced at Josie, then at the faces of the crowd. Finally he cleared his throat and said, "Maybe not because of me, no, but I do think people can change."

"Amen, brother," Cody said, moving around so that he and Carol seemed to be on Adam's side now.

"People change, but Conner Burdett?" Burke scoffed.

"Hey. Show some respect," Jason barked. "You may be Top Dawg in the wolf pack but he is still our daddy."

"Yeah, well, our *daddy* is throwing this big deal,

inviting out the town for the first and last time, to celebrate what you've done for him."

"Given him a grandson?" Adam asked.

"Brought Global here with an offer to buy out the Crumble. He doesn't know the offer will close us down and maybe be an end to the Carolina Crumble Pattie forever, but I don't think that would matter to him one bit. The old man plans to sell out first chance he gets and retire."

"That offer hasn't been formally extended." Adam went toe-to-toe with his older brother, but because of their heights it did not bring them eye to eye, literally or figuratively. "It's just one person's recommendation. The old man doesn't know for sure how it will all play out."

"He doesn't have to know how it will all play out. He knows Global is prepared to come in with a lot of money, and if it's not enough, he is prepared to ask for what he wants. He knows they want to make some kind of deal and what it could mean for us."

"Us?" Adam motioned to the people surrounding them. "Or us?" He gestured to Jason, Cody, Carol, himself then Burke, but not Josie or Nathan. She tried not to take that as a sign of his feelings.

"What it could mean to the family," he said.

Mt. Knott is my family, Josie tried to remind herself. Still, it hurt a bit to have been so obviously excluded. Whatever comfort she found in her friends and neighbors, she still longed for something more.

"What it could mean to *him,*" Burke clarified.

"What about Mt. Knott?" a man in the crowd demanded.

While another raised his voice to ask, "What about the people who still have work at the factory?"

Burke just shook his head.

"Now, wait one minute here. When I started all this I never intended…" Adam cut himself off. Again he looked at the faces of those around him, this time ending with Josie. He reached out and took her by the hand. "Actually, I never thought it through that far. I expected to blow in and out of town and not really even know the results of my efforts until I was safely back in my office."

"But you *expected* the best, right?" With her eyes, Josie begged him to confirm it. She wanted something more, both as a family and from Adam, and that had to be built on knowing that deep down, he was a good, caring man.

"I guess *best* is a relative term," he said softly.

"Not when you're talking about my relatives," Burke chimed in and not softly at all.

A few people laughed.

Josie was not one of them. "Adam, you said that after this picnic I might not want you to kiss me, but you wouldn't say why."

"Maybe he planned on putting a lot of onions on his burger." Jed's attempt to throw a little levity into the tense situation only made things worse.

People murmured.

Feet shifted in the dry grass.

Burke cocked his head and hooked his thumbs in his belt loops. To Josie it had all the earmarks of a man deciding if he wanted to take a swing at another man.

"Adam, I have to ask this." Josie took a step forward, placing herself alone with Adam in the circle created by the bystanders. "Did you want to hurt your father and family so badly that you cooked up a plan that would take down the Crumble and Mt. Knott in the process?"

"No."

"Huh." Burke's shoulders eased slightly.

"I believe you," she said.

"You do?" More than one person around them asked it out loud, but it was Adam's hoarse whisper that she answered.

"I believe that you had acted on high emotion and out of old anger and fear, and did not think through the consequences of your actions. It's not the first time you've done that."

"Ya-ya-ya."

Adam lifted his chin and narrowed his eyes in Nathan's direction.

Josie put her hand on his cheek and turned him to face her again. "That's what stray dogs do. They growl and snap at anything that seems a threat to them. And everything seems a threat to them."

He lowered his gaze and nodded.

"But you are not a stray dog."

Burke opened his mouth.

Josie glared at him.

He shut it.

"You are a man who has come to take his place in the community and be a father to his son." Josie stroked her hand along the side of his face, feeling the beginnings of late-afternoon bristle on her palm. "And no matter what happens with this business or any other in town, I know you have found your place. You have come home."

"Home." He could hardly get the word out.

"Sure. He's going to have a home no matter what. But that don't necessarily apply to the rest of us here today," came a gruff voice from the back of the crowd.

Adam looked at Burke. "I never meant for it to go this way."

"I know. And to be honest, well, it was only a matter of time until some big corporation moved in and made an offer, or came up with a competitive product that would run us out of the market, or even just waited until we put ourselves out of business." Burked took a step forward, his hand extended to his younger brother. "At least this way we may come away with enough bankroll money and what's left of our reputation to get the ball rolling on some new project."

Adam took his brother's hand, shook it once, then

used it to yank the larger man off balance and into a bear hug.

"Hey, wait a minute. I'm the hug-your-fellow-man preacher-type. Quit horning in on my territory." And with that Cody joined his brothers in the embrace.

Jason stood back a moment.

"Well, what you waiting for?" A grouchy old man's voice asked what everyone was thinking.

At first Josie thought it was Jed but when she looked, Nathan had shoved the cookie in Jed's mouth. He couldn't make a sound.

That meant...

"Get your tail in there and act like a brother, not some snarling dog." Conner slapped his next-to-youngest son on the back.

"Dad?" Jason stumbled forward, then laughed and threw his arms around the rest of the pack.

Conner came forward and did likewise.

Josie laughed with delight at the picture they made, but even as she did some small part of her ached. All her life she had yearned to be a part of a family like this, and all she had gotten was...

"Ophelia?" She squinted into the crowd right into a face that was identical to hers.

Chapter Fifteen

In two or three hurried steps, Josie reached Jed and Warren. She took Nathan in her arms. If Adam noticed, she didn't know. Her attention remained on her twin sister and the rising anxiety in her own chest.

Ophelia circled through the crowd, seemingly to give the Burdetts—and Adam—a wide berth. She had clearly spotted them all, but had she seen Josie? Had she been seeking out and found the baby that she had left in Josie's care?

"Is that…?" someone asked.

"What's *she* doing here?" Warren wanted to know.

Josie wrapped Nathan deeper into the protection of her motherly embrace. "I don't know," she managed to whisper, though her throat had gone bone dry.

"Does it matter *why* she's come?" Jed stood shoulder to shoulder with his regular counter-companion.

Warren shook his head. "Pardon me for saying it,

Josie, but in all the years we've known you, that little boy is the only good ever come from one of your sister's visits."

The baby hid his face in her shoulder and she cradled the back of his head with one hand.

"Run, Josie," someone close by hollered.

"We can detain her," Jed suggested, though from the look on his face, tangling with Ophelia was the last thing he wanted to have to do. "Run if you feel you have to."

Run? Grab her son and get out of the crowd, out of Mt. Knott? She could even lie low for a while, knowing that Ophelia would never have the patience or resources to wait her out.

Run. If the roles were reversed and she had shown up unannounced before the adoption were finalized that's exactly what Ophelia would have done. Assume the worst and protect herself.

That's the way they had both been raised. Take what you want and run with it, no matter who you have to leave in your wake, no matter who it hurts. Only it had never hurt just the ones left behind. Josie knew Ophelia still bore the scars of the times she had put instant gratification above all else.

Run? Where to? And *from* what? Josie knew that Ophelia had probably chosen this very public event for her surprise visit, because anywhere else she expected her sister would have evaded her. That she'd have done everything possible to keep Ophelia and

Nathan apart. Here, with so many people around and on the outskirts of town with no friendly home or business to duck into, Ophelia thought she would have the advantage over Josie.

But Josie knew she had the advantage. Surrounded by people Josie loved and who loved both her and her son, and with Nathan's father close at hand, her son would be all right. That's all that mattered. And besides, by allowing her to be a part of how Adam had changed and grown these past few days, the Lord had prepared Josie for this exact thing.

Does it matter why she's come? Jed's question rang again in her ears.

Josie thought of the prodigal's return that had so been on her mind of late. She remembered the stories of lost lambs and Josie had her answer.

She raised her head to see the Burdetts still talking among themselves, hugging, laughing, unaware of the small drama building on the fringes of the onlookers.

Josie knew how to respond when the lost lamb returned to the fold.

She *did* run. With Nathan in her arms she ran straight toward Ophelia.

"Phellie!" She used the special nickname she alone used for her sister. "Over here!"

"Pheenie?" Ophelia sputtered. Her expression was a clash of emotions, surprise, apprehension, defensiveness, disbelief.

Josie stopped with barely a foot between them.

Her fears reared up and made her question if she had done the right thing.

Nathan squirmed in her arms.

Josie gave him a kiss. He was safe. He was hers. And her hurting and once-lost sister had come back. If she were truly the woman of faith she wanted to be, now was the time to set her childhood fears aside and trust the Lord.

She reached out her trembling hand to Ophelia at last. "Welcome home."

Ophelia glanced down, hesitated, then took it.

The second their fingers touched Josie felt a rush of warmth and love she had not known since they were little girls together.

Ophelia must have felt it, too, as tears filled her usually cold and calculating eyes.

And just that fast they were hugging one another, Nathan between them, wriggling and giggling.

A murmur went up around them, something between a gasp of surprise and an approving cheer.

"Okay, okay. Let's get this over with—what are you doing here? How did you find us out here? And would you like to hold the baby?" Josie laughed and pulled away, facing her sister and the future at last. She sniffled and wiped away a tear from her sister's cheek, then stood back, giving her a once over. "And why are you wearing my clothes?"

Ophelia tugged at the sailor-style shirt then at the waistband of the white jeans that Josie had slipped out of, preferring the pink-and-green outfit she had on now. "I tore mine breaking into that Home Cookin' place of yours. Found these on the counter and just…"

"You broke into my business?" She tried to remember if she had put the money away properly when she had closed up last. She recalled leaving the drawer out when Adam had been there, but nothing else. "Why?"

"Because it was locked," Ophelia said as if Josie had just asked the stupidest question possible.

Josie did feel stupid. And naive. And…

"As for your other questions," Ophelia went on. "I am in town because I have a lot of unfinished business here. There are flyers about this party all over the place, and yes." She stepped forward and put her hands under Nathan's arms to lift him away from Josie. "I would very much like to hold the baby."

"Want I should call law about that break-in, Sweetie Pie?" Warren asked.

"Sweetie Pie?" Ophelia gave Warren a suspicious look. She tugged Nathan free and curled him close to her, then asked Josie, "This is your…sweetie?"

"No, that is *my* sweetie." Warren's wife stepped forward, her experience handling rude teens at the bowling alley coming in mighty handy as she met Ophelia eye to eye. "Everyone calls Josie 'Sweetie Pie' because she means so much to us and we wouldn't want to see her hurt."

Josie wanted to tell them all that her sister would

never do anything to hurt her. But she couldn't do it. She swallowed to wash back the acid sickness at the back of her throat as she studied the woman holding her—Josie's…and Ophelia's…son.

For the first time in maybe five years Ophelia did not look like an older sister to Josie. Her face was scrubbed clean and her complexion rivaled Josie's for color in her cheeks and freckles on her nose. She did not have on her usual layers of makeup, nor did she reek of cigarette smoke. She wore her hair natural again, just as Josie did. The curls falling around her shoulders, clean and free of streaks of blue, pink or wine-red. She wore no jewelry, no studs in her eyebrows or biker symbols around her neck. No black nail polish. She was not sneering.

Josie closed her eyes, waited one second, then opened again, half expecting to see something of the old Ophelia there that she had not noticed before. But no.

Not since they were kids and they had played "trick the teacher" by swapping places in the class-room had these identical twins looked so…identical.

It seemed to fascinate Nathan, who wound his chubby fingers in Ophelia's hair and singsonged his contented "Ya-ya-ya."

"Ya-ya-ya," Josie murmured, her eyes fixed on her child and hoping this would not be the time he finally formed the word *Mama.* She didn't know if she could take that. She drew a deep breath, aware of the collective breathing of the people around her. She heard some commotion, but blocked it out in order to ask what she had to ask. "What *unfinished business* do you have here?"

"Maybe we should go someplace a little more private?" Ophelia rubbed her hand over Nathan's plump leg.

Private. Josie tried to think what to do. Tried to ask the Lord for guidance, but her heart was beating so hard and her head ached. All she could think about was taking Nathan back and...

"Josie, do you want me to go get—" Warren began.

His wife interrupted with a statement aimed Ophelia's way. "Maybe everyone should stay right here while I go get the sheriff."

"No one needs to call the sheriff." Adam pushed through the ring of people, his face grim but filled with a peace that had not been there before he reconciled and accepted the forgiveness of his father and family.

For a split second relief washed over Josie. Then it dawned on her. With Ophelia's new look and with her wearing Josie's clothes, Adam might not be able to tell them apart. Even when they were separated by time and space and all sorts of experiences, Josie had worried that Adam's feelings for her were tangled up and colored by his feelings for Ophelia. Or at least by his sense of responsibility and natural concern for the woman who had carried and given life to his baby boy.

If Ophelia demanded Nathan back, it only stood

to reason Adam's attention, perhaps even his affection would follow, right?

The anguish was almost too much to bear. Ophelia's return might cost her both Nathan and Adam. She would lose everything she held dear and Ophelia would be the one to have a family at last and Josie would have nothing.

But God had brought her to this point. He had prepared her. She knew that. She could not stand there silent and put Adam to some kind of childish test; she had to speak and face what was to come with faith and hope.

Josie opened her mouth to say something.

Ophelia did the same.

"I don't want to hear it." Adam put his hand up as he spoke to Ophelia. "I have a few things to say myself. But first let me get one thing straight."

He *spoke* to Ophelia. He *approached* Ophelia.

Josie's heart ached. It actually ached. He did not know the difference between Josie and…

"Ophelia, give me my son." He took Nathan gently from her. "He belongs with his real mother."

He turned and met Josie's eyes. In one step and without taking his gaze from hers, he brought the baby to Josie.

"You knew," she whispered as she cuddled her son close.

"Ya-ya-ya."

"Of course I knew." He ran his hand over Nathan's

head, then rested it lightly on Josie's arm. "I told you that. I *know* you, Josie. The good and the bad, the sweet and the secret. I know you by the way you look at our son and by the way I feel when I look at you."

How do you feel when you look at me? She pressed her lips together to keep from blurting out the question.

Adam smiled at her, gave her arm a squeeze, then turned slightly to make eye contact with Josie's twin. "Sadly and to my own detriment, I only know Ophelia by her pain."

"Pain." Ophelia repeated the word quite softly. Not defiant and ugly as Josie expected. She nodded, her shoulders slouched slightly, as if she had slipped the word on like a yoke and was trying to decide what to do next. Finally she took off the yoke, humbled herself and said, "I didn't come to try to take Nathan away from you, Josie."

"You didn't?" Josie's own burden lifted. "I mean, I didn't think you had. I *hoped* you hadn't, but…"

"But I hadn't given you a lot of reasons to trust me up until now." Ophelia reached out and tugged on the lace of Nathan's shoe.

"I always wanted to…trust you, Phellie. I always wanted to."

"And now I want to be worthy of your trust, Pheenie. I came here now to make sure everything was all right."

"By breaking into my place of business?"

"I didn't know how to find your house. I'm not from here, remember?"

Josie thought of telling her that she could have just asked anyone, but then remembered that everyone, including Bingo and his little red scooter was out here.

"So I figured Josie's Home Cookin' Kitchen was the best place to wait for you."

"So you broke in?"

She shrugged. "Old habits die hard. And I did it for a good reason. I needed to see you."

"Yeah?" Josie tried keep her hope on a leash. Her sister had a way of making big deals out of nothing and acting as if the most important things were of no consequence whatsoever.

"See, that private eye you hired spoke to Mom, who tracked me down, set things in motion. Made me think. I'd done this one good thing, but hadn't really done it right." She pushed her hair back. She cocked one hip, then swept the back of her hand along Nathan's cheek. "I finally found where Adam had got to and tried to contact him to tell him about the baby. When I learned he'd gone back to Mt. Knott, I felt I had to come. I was afraid he'd try to take Nathan away from you."

"It did cross my mind," he admitted. "At first. Then I saw Nathan with Josie and…"

"Da-da!" Nathan yelled.

"And I knew that's where he belonged," Adam finished, never looking away from Josie.

Did she dare believe what she saw in his eyes? Or

was the emotion of the moment coloring her perception? Josie struggled to keep her voice strong as she tore her gaze away from Adam's and spoke to her sister. "I thought when my letter to you came back returned…"

"I don't know about a letter, but I moved out of my old place. Too many temptations. I'm in a program now at a church."

"You've accepted Christ?" Josie took a joyous step toward her sister.

"I, uh, I'm opening up to it," was all Ophelia would say. "It's just a lot to do alone, you know? Stay sober. Overcome a lifetime of selfishness? How do you do that?"

"You started when you decided to have Nathan," Josie said.

"Something I feel I can never thank you enough for," Adam added, his head bowed slightly in a show of gratitude and humility. "Thank you, Ophelia, for not compounding *our* selfishness. For having Nathan *and* giving him to a person who would love him no matter where he came from, who would make a home for him, no matter what personal sacrifices she had to make."

Adam touched Josie's arm, pride and happiness shining from deep within his eyes. "Josie, I… You… Thank you. Not just for what you did for my son but what you've done for me. The things you've made me realize, the way you've helped me look at my world…I…"

Josie held her breath.

"My brain tells me it's too soon to say this, but it's really how I feel." Adam moved close to her and took one of her hands in both of his. "I love you, Josie."

"Wooo-hooo!" Jed led the cheer that went up through the crowd, when they all began to laugh afterward, even Ophelia joined in.

"Now, you say it back to him, Sweetie Pie," Warren prodded in a teasingly loud whisper.

Josie wanted to say it, but her voice failed her, so she mouthed it instead. *I love you, too.*

Another whoop.

Adam broke into laughter and pulled her into his arms, kissing her temple, her cheek, then lightly, her lips.

The crowd showed their approval with applause this time.

Adam kissed her again, this time on the forehead; then he kissed Nathan on the head, as well, before he took a deep breath and looked at Ophelia. His expression changed to guarded kindness. "I have something more to ask you, Ophelia."

Ophelia dropped her gaze downward. She spoke softly, guessing, "Why didn't I tell you about Nathan sooner?"

"No." He shook his head and stepped away from Josie to face Ophelia fully, sincerely, humbly. "Can you ever forgive me?"

"What?"

He reached out and took her by the hand. "I'm asking for your forgiveness."

Josie's heart swelled.

"But…but why?" Ophelia looked past the man and found Josie and Nathan.

"Because it's what families do," Josie explained, choking back a sob. "It's what happens when the lost lamb returns to the fold. We try to make things so they don't stray again. God loves us and forgives us and so we—we do the same for others."

Ophelia's face went blank, no doubt as she tried to process it all.

Josie marveled that she, herself, did not burst into tears. *A family.* An unconventional one, to be sure, but if Ophelia forgave Adam and was open to talking to the two of them, a family they would be.

Adam cleared his throat, which by his standards was probably close to a total emotional breakdown, she suspected.

"Oh, forgive him already! I couldn't stand it if you didn't." Jed scrunched up his whole face, trying to look annoyed, but was unable to hide his emotional investment in it all.

Warren pulled out the red hankie and blew his nose, good and noisy.

Josie laughed. She couldn't help herself. Adam loved her! He'd made amends with his family. Nathan was going to be hers legally. Ophelia had returned and was open to trying a new way of life.

Sure, the Crumble might still close. Her business might fall as a result. She and Adam might not work out or have a long-term relationship beyond their connection to Nathan, but Josie had the thing she had longed for all her life....

"What do you have to be so happy about?" Ophelia asked.

Josie threw her arms around her sister and gave her a hug, with Nathan still in her arms. "Because I have family. And for the first time I can recall I feel like nothing is going to take that away from me."

Chapter Sixteen

By the first week of November all the leaves had changed to brilliant orange, yellow and red. Some had begun to fall, making a trip down a winding mountain road feel like a trip through a confetti-strewn parade route.

Why not? Josie felt she had so much to celebrate.

She strolled to the front door of the Home Cookin' Kitchen, then turned to look at the prayer list on the wall.

Among the requests for health and job security now read the words Josie never thought she'd see:

"Pray for the Burdett family as they make their big decision." Warren had been the first to sign that one. Jed next. Then Josie. The list grew and grew and even included Elvie Maloney and Micah Applebee, only two of the most high-profile of the Burdetts' detractors.

Adam had come last night with his camera phone

and taken a photo of the wall scrawled floor to ceiling with names.

"I want to carry this into the meeting," he had told Josie with a kiss to her cheek.

Josie had returned it with a kiss to his lips. She thought that was a completely acceptable way to send her sweetie off to the meeting that would determine the fate of the family business. Global had done something called a "due diligence." Conner complained they'd come in and pulled records and files and snooped around everything except their medicine cabinets. Today they would present their offer to the board. Adam was just sitting in as a guest and advisor, but with so much at stake they were all anxious.

The sky had gotten overcast throughout the morning. It threatened to drizzle any minute now. The wind kicked up, and Josie watched a few leaves tumble down from the nearest tree.

Bingo beeped, and she went out to meet him, shivering as she did.

"Sorry, Sweetie Pie, bills mostly but there is one here from your sister."

"Thanks, Bingo."

"Hope it's good news."

"Me, too." Josie would save that letter for later. Ophelia had had a setback, but after spending a lot of time with Carol and Cody Burdett, had gone into a residential Christian rehab program.

She thumbed through the rest of the envelopes.

Bingo peered over her shoulder, probably hoping she would read her sister's letter and share all the news.

"Nothing new on the adoption," he told her. "Not that I read your mail, you know, but I got to—"

"I know, read the outsides to know what to deliver." Josie laughed, thanked him and hurried back inside to get out of the autumn chill.

The lack of information did not worry her. The adoption process was well underway and Adam…

Josie looked at the phone and held her breath. This had been one of the longest mornings of her life. The coffee commuters had already come and gone, and she'd even had time to clear away their mess and count up the proceeds. For once the amount not only covered her costs, it gave her enough left over to buy herself a cup of coffee— and not one of her own, the fancy kind in a city coffee shop.

She had counted that twice, then taken some fresh pies out of the oven and served them to the regulars, who gobbled them up, each making comments about her secret ingredient. They'd noticed it this time because Josie had been leaving it out. Or experimenting with different things trying to come up with a substitute. But today, with the Crumble on the line, it only seemed right she'd make her pies with the Carolina Crumble Pattie mixed into the top crust.

Adam should have called with some news by now.

"You ever tell anyone that secret?" Jed poked the last bite of his pie into his mouth.

"What secret?" Warren scraped up the last of the cherry filling on his plate with the side of his fork. "Only secret she's keeping is when she's going to wise up, toss over that Burdett and run off and marry me."

"You old fool. Who in their right mind would toss over a strapping young fellow with a great big inheritance burning a hole in his pocket, just waiting to get reinvested right here in Mt. Knott, for a broken-down ol' pie hog like you?" Jed laughed.

"He really going to invest in Mt. Knott no matter which way the vote goes at the Crumble, Miss Josie?" Warren wiped his mouth then took a sip of coffee.

"That's what he says," she confirmed.

"Good for him."

"Good for us," Jed threw in. "'Cuz if the Crumble goes…"

If the Crumble went—meaning the Burdetts sold out and Global shut them down and restricted them using the recipe ever again—then it didn't matter how much money Adam invested in the town, Josie's pies would never be the same. And she couldn't help wondering what would become of other parts of her life?

R-rr-rr-ring!

Josie jumped.

"That might be the call." Warren slapped his hand on the counter.

"You think so, Captain Obvious?" Jed nudged him with his elbow.

"Hello?" Josie held her breath, expecting to hear Adam on the other end. "Oh," was all she could muster when she heard the voice of the paper-goods rep on the other end, wanting to know if she needed to place an order. "Nope. Sorry, I still have a bit left over from the barbecue."

"Not him?" Jed asked.

"Now who's Captain Obvious?" Warren wanted to know, before he added to cheer Josie up, "Won't be long now."

"Can't draw it out forever," Jed agreed.

"How long can it take to plan out the future of one family and a whole townful of fine folks?"

"Adam!" It was as if a light had been flicked on and her whole day had turned bright just to see him standing there. She ran to him and threw her arms around his neck. "What do you know? What did they decide? What happened? Tell me the good news first, okay, sweetie?"

"Yeah, sweetie, tell us the good news first," Jed and Warren chimed in unison.

"The good news?" Adam's dark eyes sparkled. He touched Josie's hair, stroked his thumb along her jaw, then placed a kiss on the tip of her nose. "Well,

I was going to save this for a more-private time, but if you want the good news first…"

"Hurry up!" she demanded, knowing he was toying with her.

"Okay." He nodded then dropped to one knee before her.

"What?" She looked down at him, confused and more than a little excited. "What are you—"

"Shhh. You asked me to tell you the good news first, right?"

"Right."

"The good news is that I plan to take care of you and Nathan for the rest of your lives, no matter what happens at the Crumble or with our extended families. And toward that end—" he reached inside his black leather jacket and pulled free a small red velvet box "—Josie Redmond, will you marry me?"

Josie held her breath. She had imagined him coming in here and telling her everything from they had saved the business to telling her he had to ride off on his Harley, never to return. But this?

"M-marry you?"

"You know what this means, don't you?" Jed asked his counter mate.

"Yup. That she is never ever going to wise up and marry me." Warren sulked, then brightened. "Although, my wife will probably appreciate that news to no end."

"No, you fool, it means that them Burdetts sold

out the Crumble. If they didn't, he wouldn't want to propose first, he'd have told her the good news up front."

Josie put her hand to her throat. "Is that an accurate assessment of things?"

"Has anything those guys come up with ever been accurate?" Adam's smile grew, slowly at first, then spread wide until he couldn't contain a roll of joyous laughter. "We did it, Josie."

"We…did?"

"The family turned down the buyout."

"Yee-hooo!" Jed hollered.

"Well, I'll be!" Warren shook his head.

"But why? How? What's to keep the place from bottoming out and going bankrupt?"

"New blood."

She winced. "What?"

He took both her hands in his. "We have a third party, new investor. Came in at the eleventh hour with some great ideas for restructuring, starting some new product lines and running the business based on Biblical principles."

"Biblical?" Josie had heard Adam and the brothers discussing that before. "And this new investor…"

"Wants to partner with the family. One member of the family more than others, I suspect"

She shook her head. Nothing he had said since the proposal had really sunk in. "I don't…"

"Dora Hoag. My old boss."

"Oh!" Josie laughed at last.

"*That* made sense to you?"

"Love always makes sense to me." She put her arms around his neck.

"Then you are a wiser person than I am, Josie, because love has had me baffled until I met you."

She went up on tiptoe and kissed him.

"Does that mean she's accepting his proposal?" Jed asked.

"Yep. Get out your Sunday best, you old fool, looks like you and me are going to be flower girls."

And they were.

Not flower girls, but they did have the responsibility of bringing Nathan down the aisle and holding him there to bear witness to the marriage of his parents.

Everyone they loved was there, Ophelia, Conner, Burke, Jason, Cody and Carol. And Bingo. And even Dora came.

And when the minister pronounced them man and wife, Nathan wasn't afraid to put in his two cents. "Dada! Mama! Ya-ya-ya!"

* * * * *

Dear Reader,

As a parent, I have long understood the father's rejoicing at the return of the prodigal son. As a former air force "brat" who grew up to be a social worker, I've always tried to work hard, respect others, consider the greater good and be a team player. I've seen people who did none of the above rise to the top and reap what seemed like abundant rewards, while I worked away unnoticed in the background. Because of that, I definitely see the point of the brother who had remained with his father, working and being obedient.

But as I grew older, I began to think about the nature of forgiveness and family and wondered what it must feel like to be the one on the receiving end of that rejoicing and forgiveness. I know how it feels to accept and be grateful for these good gifts from the Lord, of course. But given human nature, I suspected it was a much different feeling coming from another human, especially one as close as a family member, where there are so many issues built into the relationship.

And so came the story of *Somebody's Baby.* A story of family and forgiveness and the hope and joy that comes when a lamb is returned to the fold. I hope you enjoy it.

Annie Jones

QUESTIONS FOR DISCUSSION

1. Josie had to deal with coming from a family that did not support her faith. How can Christians deal with loved ones who reject their faith?

2. How can Christians reach out to those who have no family support to help them in their walk with the Lord?

3. Adam took his inheritance and his share of the family business and, in a manner of speaking, re-invented himself. If you were to receive a windfall, what would you do with it?

4. Would you like to live in a small town like Mt. Knott? Why or why not?

5. Josie was known for her special pie crust. Do you have a recipe that you are known for? Do you keep it a secret? Whom would you share it with?

6. Do you know any twins? How do you tell them apart? What makes them different from each other?

7. When his mother died, Adam felt he lost the one person who truly accepted him. Have you ever felt all alone in the world? How did you overcome that?

8. Mt. Knott is a tight-knit community. Does your community offer you prayer and encouragement? Are there ways that you could offer that to others?

9. In the end, several characters have to ask for and also give forgiveness for their behavior. Many times we do not get to speak directly to those we forgive or they to us when we need to be forgiven. Do you think that asking for and openly giving forgiveness changes the nature of the act? Makes it harder or easier to follow through on?

10. Do you think it's more difficult to accept human forgiveness than divine forgiveness? Why or why not?

*Look for Burke and Dora's story
coming in 2008 from Love Inspired.
And turn the page for a preview of
THE BAREFOOT BELIEVERS
by Annie Jones
available in March 2008
from Steeple Hill books.*

"What?"

"Florida."

"Florida?"

"The cottage." Jo's heels clacked soft and swift over the floor as she went to her sister's side. "We've been saying we need to get down there and go through things. Decide what to do with it all, with the place." *Sell.* That was the solution to her situation. One big sale, one sudden influx of cash and she'd be on top again. "Perfect."

"It's worth some thought, I guess. It would get me away from…" Instead of finishing her thought Kate looked around the room, her expression sour.

"Here." Jo caught her sister by the elbow. "Let's get you settled down and comfortable."

"Pick one." Kate dumped her cane onto the love seat and hopped around the side of it, trying to avoid hitting her broken foot. "I can be settled down or I can be comfortable. I can't be both."

Jo knew what her always restless sister meant, but with this new idea burning through her thought process she did not have time for empathy. "Sit. I'll get you some water so you can take your meds, and the TV remote so you can stick your foot up on the coffee table and yell at the world."

In a matter of minutes Jo's French-manicured nails clattered over the keyboard of her laptop.

Florida real estate.

Property values.

Length of time on the market.

In a chair a few feet away, Kate flicked through the one hundred plus TV channels so fast that it created an almost strobe-light effect.

Crime show.

Crime show.

Crime show.

"If I have to spend the next three weeks watching this junk I may go insane and do bodily harm to somebody." Another click, this time to a commercial—for a crime show. "Fortunately with all these forensic science shows, I'll know how to do it without getting caught."

"Well, if you want to spare yourself the trouble of having to plan the perfect crime, there's always Florida."

"We'll always have Florida, kid," she said with a very bad Humphrey Bogart impression.

"Not if I have my way we won't," Jo muttered under her breath and double clicked the mouse to scan yet another site on the hottest selling properties along the Gulf coast.

"What was that?"

Jo glanced up. "I, uh, it's just that it's sat empty for two years now because no one rented it. Not sure what that means or what shape it's in, but this opportunity *has* presented itself…"

"My losing the use of my foot is an opportunity?"

"The Lord works in mysterious ways." It was a pat answer, but not an altogether glib one. Kate and Jo were women of faith. Not particularly strong or studied faith, but both of them had accepted Christ as their personal Savior while still teens. And hadn't Jo been praying and praying for some kind of resolution to the mess she had found herself in? Why couldn't this be the answer?

Of course to get to that answer, she just might have to go through her sister.

R-r-r-i-i-n-n-g. The phone cut through her scheming, um, musings and jarred her into reacting.

"I'm not here!" she shouted, even as Kate thrust out her own hand in the "get thee away from me" position and said the same. "I'm not here."

Jo raised her head and met her sister's eyes. "If you're not here then where are you?"

R-r-r-i-i-n-n-g.

"Florida?" Kate ventured meekly.

Jo smiled and signed off the Internet with a decisive click. That was it. The answer to her prayer. And all she had to do to achieve it was convince her sister to dump the family home, the only thing besides the whole foot-recovery situation still holding their family together. "But this time tomorrow we'll be sitting on the veranda and sipping sweet tea, in Florida."

REQUEST YOUR FREE BOOKS!

2 FREE INSPIRATIONAL NOVELS
PLUS 2
FREE
MYSTERY GIFTS

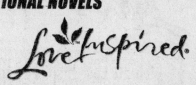

YES! Please send me 2 FREE Love Inspired® novels and my 2 FREE
mystery gifts. After receiving them, if I don't wish to receive any more books,
I can return the shipping statement marked "cancel." If I don't cancel, I will
receive 4 brand-new novels every month and be billed just $3.99 per book in
the U.S., or $4.74 per book in Canada, plus 25¢ shipping and handling per
book and applicable taxes, if any*. That's a savings of 20% off the cover price!
I understand that accepting the 2 free books and gifts places me under no
obligation to buy anything. I can always return a shipment and cancel at any
time. Even if I never buy another book from Steeple Hill, the two free books
and gifts are mine to keep forever.

113 IDN EF26 313 IDN EF27

Name	(PLEASE PRINT)	
Address		Apt. #
City	State/Prov.	Zip/Postal Code

Signature (if under 18, a parent or guardian must sign)

Order online at www.LoveInspiredBooks.com

Or mail to Steeple Hill Reader Service™:

IN U.S.A.: P.O. Box 1867, Buffalo, NY 14240-1867
IN CANADA: P.O. Box 609, Fort Erie, Ontario L2A 5X3

Not valid to current Love Inspired subscribers.

Want to try two free books from another series?
Call 1-800-873-8635 or visit www.morefreebooks.com

* Terms and prices subject to change without notice. NY residents add applicable sales
tax. Canadian residents will be charged applicable provincial taxes and GST. This offer is
limited to one order per household. All orders subject to approval. Credit or debit balances
in a customer's account(s) may be offset by any other outstanding balance owed by or to
the customer. Please allow 4 to 6 weeks for delivery.

Your Privacy: Steeple Hill is committed to protecting your privacy. Our Privacy
Policy is available online at www.eHarlequin.com or upon request from the Reader
Service. From time to time we make our lists of customers available to reputable
firms who may have a product or service of interest to you. If you would
prefer we not share your name and address, please check here. ☐

LIREG07

TITLES AVAILABLE NEXT MONTH

Don't miss these four stories in October

SLEEPING BEAUTY by Judy Baer
Suze Charles had been sleepwalking her way through life, until
she met Dr. David Grant. The sleep specialist offered her hope
for a cure—and for lasting love. But could a man who liked order
ever fit in to the menagerie that was Suze's life?

LITTLE MISS MATCHMAKER by Dana Corbit
A Tiny Blessings Tale

While dealing with a shocking revelation about his family,
firefighter Alex Donovan finds himself temporary guardian to
his cousin's children. Teacher Dinah Fraser offers to help him
learn to cope and finds herself falling for the unlikely family man.

A SEASON OF FORGIVENESS by Brenda Coulter
Her life was calm and predictable, and Victoria Talcott liked it that
way. She didn't need daredevil Sam McGarry swooping in to save
her all the time. But he always seemed to be there, rescuing her
and setting off sparks in her heart.

OPERATION: MARRIED BY CHRISTMAS by Debra Clopton
Mule Hollow's notorious runaway bride, Haley Bell Thornton,
was back. And, not surprisingly, running from another wedding.
That gave the matchmaking ladies of the town a secret holiday
plan—make wedding bells chime by Christmas for Haley and
Will Sutton, the first of her ditched fiancés.

LICNM0907